GAURAV RAJPUROHIT

THE DICTATIVE THE SLEUTH
# FORTY SEVEN
MURDER   MYSTERY   GODLY

NewDelhi • London

**BLUEROSE PUBLISHERS**
India | U.K.

Copyright © Gaurav Rajpurohit 2024

All rights reserved by author. No part of this publication may be reproduced, stored in a retrieval system or transmitted in any form or by any means, electronic, mechanical, photocopying, recording or otherwise, without the prior permission of the author. Although every precaution has been taken to verify the accuracy of the information contained herein, the publisher assumes no responsibility for any errors or omissions. No liability is assumed for damages that may result from the use of information contained within.

BlueRose Publishers takes no responsibility for any damages, losses, or liabilities that may arise from the use or misuse of the information, products, or services provided in this publication.

For permissions requests or inquiries regarding this publication, please contact:

BLUEROSE PUBLISHERS
www.BlueRoseONE.com
info@bluerosepublishers.com
+91 8882 898 898
+4407342408967

ISBN: 978-93-5989-033-3

Cover design: Yash Singhal
Typesetting: Namrata Saini

First Edition: January 2025

*To*

*My*

*Devotion*

*&*

*Worship.*

# **Acknowledgement**

My world had been a strange place but thanks to people who wanted me to build and lead others. What makes it even better that there were some people who liked my ideas and the way I was and who shared their gift of their time to mentor me. Thanks to everyone who struggle to grow and help others grow.

I owe to the teachers who have told me such wise things about life, universe, time, their origins and how to live with them. I would like to thank NMS Sir and MSC Sir (Hitmen of my life), NKC Sir, AG Sir, AC Sir, SJ Sir, DS Sir, SS Sir and NS sir for sharing their precious knowledge of physics, chemistry, maths and identifying my true identity in my Kota stream foundation. I would not be able to take this knowledge further without the help of Dashrathraj Shetty Sir, SAR Mam, Sowmya Mam, Shwetha Shetty Mam and Susan Varghese Mam in my MIT Manipal college.

I would not be able to get my book complete without the continual support and vision of my editor, Mansi chouhan. I would like to acknowledge people of BlueRose Publishers for their constant support and work.

I would like to thank my father Shankar Singh Ji Rajpurohit for being with me even when he didn't want it. Lastly I would like to thank my friends specially Mohit Joon (MJ), Lokendra Singh Rathore (Loki), Shivam Singh and my beautiful wife Deepika Rajpurohit.

# Preface

What inspired me to write this book is a one simple word "DREAM." I personally believe that "Dreams are the keys to one's success."

We should "pray" like our dreams become real dreams.

We should "exercise" like our dreams become a reality.

We should "work" like we are dreaming in reality.

We should "build" like whatever we want in our life becomes a reality.

Lastly we should "lead" like we are fulfilling our people's dreams into reality.

I always wanted to be an IITIAN but I was not selected in its entrance test. It was my dream. But through the help of my mentors I made this dream a reality. And this dream will be my next book's theme.

# Contents

Prologue .................................................. 1

The Disappearance of Jordan Naudet .................... 4

Introducing Detective Edward (47) ...................... 11

The Murder Case Unfolds ................................. 16

Introducing Marco Douglas and the Game of
Cat and Mouse ........................................... 23

Edward's Inner Circle and Family Life ................ 33

The First Major Clue – The Protruding Finger .... 41

Close Call and Rising Tensions ........................... 52

Love Romance & Relationship ............................ 59

Anna Thomas and Cathy Ron Join the Team ..... 66

Edward's Growing Bond with Joshua ................. 73

Uncovering Naudet's World ............................... 80

The Symbol .................................................. 96

The National Rally for Jordan Naudet ............... 107

The Media's Role: Anna Thomas and
Areus News .................................................. 114

The People's Movement .................................. 121

The Burning Man and The Unraveling ............. 128

Inferno and Pursuit ............................................ 139
The Weight of Knowledge ................................. 150
A Moment of Solitude ....................................... 160
Dream into Reality ............................................ 166
The Unveiling American Dream ....................... 173
The Buried Truth .............................................. 183
The Unmasking ................................................. 191
The Fall of Marco Douglas ................................ 198
The Final Farewell ............................................ 205
Epilogue: A Full Circle ...................................... 212

# Prologue

"1...2...3...**4**...5...6...**7**..."

Each number hung in the air, pregnant with significance. To some, they were mere digits, devoid of meaning. But to those attuned to the subtle rhythms of life, each number held a secret, a mystery waiting to be unraveled.

Mr. James Bean, the head of Scotland Christian School, had an unusual obsession—cinema. His love for films wasn't just a passing interest; it was an all-consuming passion. From silent classics to modern thrillers, his knowledge spanned genres and decades. His office, otherwise filled with academic texts, had an entire shelf dedicated to DVDs, Blu-rays, and special edition box sets.

To most, Mr. Bean was a stoic and disciplined headmaster, known for his firm management of the prestigious school. But those who knew him well understood that beneath the strict exterior was a cinephile who could passionately discuss Hitchcock's suspenseful frames or Coppola's narrative depths.

One quiet evening, as autumn's chill began to settle in, he encountered something new. A colleague had mentioned a movie over lunch—a film so captivating, so layered, that it had left viewers stunned.

"You're always on the hunt for something different, James," the teacher had said. "This one's called *47*. It might just be your next obsession."

Intrigued, James sat in his office that night, browsing his streaming service until he found it—a simple poster with a stark number: *47*. Beneath it, a tagline read, "One man's ambition leads to a deadly game of power."

The synopsis unfolded on screen:

"*47*—Business magnate Jordan Naudet, the powerful owner of Alliance, a multinational energy corporation, is found missing after a mysterious disappearance. A private detective, known only as *47*, is hired to uncover the truth behind Naudet's murder. In a tale of power, greed, and betrayal, secrets are buried deep—just like the victim."

James felt a thrill of excitement. "This," he muttered, "is what I've been looking for."

As the film began, the screen revealed a moonlit park. A tall, distinguished man stood with his back to the camera, cradling a cat. The atmosphere felt calm until a gunshot shattered the silence. The man collapsed, his cat fleeing into the night. The camera zoomed in, revealing his pained expression and the

Bible he tried to reach before succumbing to his injuries. The screen cut to black.

Mr. Bean leaned forward, eyes glued to the screen. "Well, this is going to be interesting," he whispered.

The title card *47* appeared, setting the stage for what he knew was more than just another crime film.

# The Disappearance of Jordan Naudet

The night was cold and still, the kind of night that seemed to swallow sound. The moon, veiled by a scattering of clouds, barely illuminated the deserted park where Jordan Naudet, a man of ambition and mystery, walked with his beloved cat, Whiskers. Naudet had always believed in a unique life philosophy that intrigued many: "The life you've always wanted is buried beneath everything you already have." This belief wasn't just a mantra but a driving force in his life, a constant reminder to never stop digging, to never stop striving, no matter the cost.

Yet, on that cold evening, as he ambled through the park, the future he had so diligently crafted slipped away without warning. As he walked beneath the ancient oaks and the ever-silent park benches, his thoughts swirled with ideas of greatness, of conquests, of untold secrets buried beneath the mundane routines of his life. Whiskers, his white Persian cat, trotted beside him, occasionally stopping to sniff the ground. Little did they know, they were not alone.

## Forty Seven (47)

The park, once a place of solitude and comfort for Naudet, had become a stage for something far darker. From the shadows of the trees, a single figure watched, patient and still. The sound of footsteps behind him remained unnoticed by Naudet, consumed as he was by his reflections on the future. A sudden crack broke the silence—an unmistakable sound of a gunshot. The bullet found its mark, and in an instant, Jordan Naudet, the man who had once believed that everything he needed was hidden beneath his possessions, fell lifeless to the ground.

His final breath was shallow, his thoughts drifting not toward his ambitions, but to the faces of his family—his parents, his sister, his ancestors, who had shaped him into the man he had become. He thought of them just as life slipped away, as his mind flickered to memories he would never be able to touch again. The bullet had been swift, its trajectory precise, and before Naudet could even process the pain, his life was stolen from him.

The murderer, cloaked in the darkness, wasted no time. The world would never know what had happened in that park—no one would see the flash of the gun or the vanishing figure retreating into the shadows. Naudet's body would not be found for days, buried in an unmarked grave, discarded like a forgotten item from a past life. The only trace of his existence would be the zippered Bible he carried with him, the small personal symbol of his holistic nature and his devotion to a higher power. It remained clenched in his cold hands, its pages soaked in the final moments of his life, a silent testament to his unyielding belief in the unseen truths of the universe.

## **Four Days Later**

Four days passed before anyone realized that Jordan Naudet was truly missing. At first, his family had hoped that he was simply out of reach, perhaps on one of his spontaneous trips to "find himself" as he often did. But when the days stretched on without a word, the family's hope began to fray at the edges. His sister, Isabelle, knew something was wrong. Naudet's sister, Isabelle, flew in from Paris the next morning, her face pale and tight with worry. She had always been close with her brother, even though they led vastly different lives. Isabelle was an artist, a painter who had spent her life avoiding the corporate world that Jordan thrived in. But despite their differences, they were family, and Isabelle adored him.

Panic began to set in, and soon the Naudet family made the decision to offer a reward for any information about his disappearance.

The phone lines began to ring incessantly, each call a new lead, some promising, others nothing more than false hopes and dead ends. The family's desperation grew as they sifted through the lies that poured in. No one knew where Jordan Naudet was, and even worse—no one seemed to care. It was as if he had simply vanished from the earth.

In the midst of this chaos, a solution appeared—one that had become an almost mythical name in investigative circles. Edward Lucas, known to all as "47," was a private detective with a reputation that stretched across cities, countries, and continents. The name was enough to make criminals shiver and law enforcement officials look up in reverence. For 47, there was no case too complex, no mystery too obscure. He had a reputation for seeing things others couldn't, for diving deep into situations that others deemed impossible to solve.

It was a crisp afternoon when Edward Lucas received the call that would pull him into one of the most confounding cases of his career. He was sitting at a small café in downtown Seattle, nursing his usual—black coffee, no sugar—while skimming through the latest headlines on his tablet. His sharp, calculating eyes scanned the text with the efficiency of a machine, absorbing information, cross-referencing details, and storing away useful tidbits in the recesses of his mind. He liked to call this process "DrEaMing"—Drinking, Eating, and Mobilizing his thoughts simultaneously. A ritual that, over the years, had become second nature to him.

As soon as the Naudet family reached out to him, 47 agreed to take the case, though he never asked for the reward money. He wasn't in it for the cash or the fame. He had his own reasons for taking on cases that others dismissed as unsolvable, but none of that mattered now. He had a man to find.

47 wasn't alone in this endeavor. Over the years, he had built a small but formidable team—his two closest allies, brothers Rudradev Singh and Loganathan Singh. Rudra and Logan were not just partners in crime-solving; they were family, bound by blood and loyalty. The duo had been through countless cases together, and their unique dynamic had earned them the nickname "Bhartiya Brothers" (Brothers belonging to India).No criminal ever escaped them, and no case was too challenging for their combined efforts.

Rudra, the elder of the two brothers, was a tactical genius, always thinking several steps ahead. Logan, the younger sibling, had a knack for connecting seemingly unrelated pieces of information, a skill that had proven invaluable in many cases. Together with 47, they formed an unstoppable team, each of them bringing their own expertise to the table.

The day after 47 accepted the case, he gathered his team. They met at his office—a nondescript building tucked away in a quiet corner of the city. The walls were covered with maps, charts, and photographs. There was a sense of organized chaos, but to 47, everything had its place.

"Alright," 47 said, his voice steady as always. "We have a case. Jordan Naudet is missing, presumed dead. No one knows what happened to him, but the family's desperate. They offered a reward, and now we're on the clock."

Rudra leaned back in his chair, his fingers tapping rhythmically on the armrest. "What do we know so far? Who's involved?"

"Not much," 47 replied. "Naudet was last seen alive in a park, walking his cat. Witnesses say nothing unusual happened. No one heard anything, no one saw anything. But we know something's off."

Logan sat forward, his eyes narrowing. "We're looking at a clean job. Whoever did this knew exactly what they were doing. No traces, no witnesses. Whoever murdered him wanted him gone without leaving a trace."

"Exactly," 47 nodded. "We'll start with the family—interview them, get a sense of who he was. We need to understand the man before we can understand the case."

The next few days were a whirlwind of interviews and investigations. 47, Rudra, and Logan dug deep into Naudet's life, piecing together fragments of his past, his business dealings, his family dynamics. They learned that Naudet was not just a businessman but a man driven by a deep philosophical belief. His life was a complex web of ambition, spirituality, and personal ties, all of which seemed to intersect in strange ways. But none of it made sense.

No one had any idea why someone would want to kill him, and the deeper they dug, the more questions they uncovered. Naudet's family was just as perplexed—his sister, Isabelle, was devastated but had no answers to offer. She had never known her brother to have enemies, and yet, the more they spoke to her, the more they felt something was off. Naudet's odd belief, his mysterious nature, and his enigmatic lifestyle—was there something hidden beneath the surface? Something that had made him a target?

The search for Jordan Naudet had begun, and with each passing day, 47, Rudra, and Logan could feel the case becoming darker, more twisted, and far more complicated than they had ever imagined.

But one thing was clear: they would find him. They had to.

# Introducing Detective Edward (47)

Detective Edward Lucas, known in certain circles simply as "47," stood in his dimly lit office, eyes fixed on a board covered with case files and evidence. His workspace had an almost ritualistic air, meticulously organized, with every item intentionally placed. Along the walls, a collage of clues painted a picture of Jordan Naudet's life and the tangled web of secrets surrounding his death.

On the board, a large photo of Jordan Naudet stared back at him — a confident, ambitious man in his prime, now reduced to a crime scene file. Edward's gaze shifted, taking in the newspaper clippings, snippets of Naudet's speeches, and snapshots of the late businessman at various events. Red strings connected pieces of information in a complex network that only Edward fully understood. For others, the board might look like a mess of tangled thoughts, but for him, it was a map leading to the truth.

Edward's expression was tense, his brow furrowed in concentration. He approached the board, his fingers tracing the edges of a photo where Naudet stood with a man he didn't recognize. A new thread to follow, he thought, adding a question mark beside it. His mind raced with possibilities, weaving in and out of known facts and unexplored theories.

The hum of the small clock in the corner ticked away, but Edward paid no mind. Time meant little when he was immersed like this. Solving cases was not just work for him; it was a calling. His code name, *47,* symbolized his resolve to take on tasks that others shied away from, missions that required more than just skill but a sense of purpose and strength. Strength not just from within but, as he often said, "from above." He'd come to rely on this deeper sense of faith in the face of darkness, a commitment to justice he attributed to something greater than himself.

As he pinned another photograph to the board, his mind ran through each piece of information like a well-rehearsed script. He closed his eyes briefly, collecting his thoughts, trying to bridge the gap between the known and the unknown. If Naudet's death had been as clean as it looked, why had certain people taken an unusual interest in closing the case so quickly? And who benefited most from Naudet being out of the picture?

The door to Edward's office creaked open, and in walked his closest allies — Rudra Singh and

## Forty Seven (47)

Loganathan "Logan" Singh, known to him as "The Last Ride Brothers". The nickname was born of their shared experiences bringing notorious criminals to justice, often being the last faces those criminals saw before being carted off. Rudra and Logan had been by his side for years, and though they differed in personality, both shared a sense of loyalty to Edward's cause.

"Still staring at that board, Ed? Thought you'd cracked this case by now," Logan said, smirking as he looked over the room. His eyes quickly scanned the board, assessing the connections with the keen eye of a strategist.

Edward didn't look up. "I've cracked pieces of it, Logan. But pieces don't solve murders. It's like finding a puzzle with half the pieces missing."

Rudra leaned against the wall, his arms crossed. Unlike Logan's sharp tongue, Rudra's demeanor was calm and centered. He didn't say much unless necessary, but when he did, his words carried weight. "We have to find those missing pieces, then," he said simply, his gaze fixed on Edward. "You wouldn't let this go unfinished."

"No, I won't," Edward replied, his tone steady but intense. He turned to face his friends, grateful for their presence. They'd gone through thick and thin together, and in each of them, he found different strengths that complemented his own. Rudra's quiet wisdom grounded him, and Logan's analytical mind pushed him to consider angles he might otherwise miss.

Rudra broke the silence, his voice lower. "This is more than just a job, Edward. This one's personal for you. Isn't it?"

Edward didn't answer immediately, but he could feel their gaze. They knew him well enough to read between the lines.

"You know me, Rudra," he finally replied, the flicker of a smile crossing his face. "It's not just about solving crimes. It's about justice. And sometimes..." He paused, feeling the weight of his words. "Sometimes, you need more than your own strength to find it."

Rudra nodded. He understood. The concept of relying on "God's strength" wasn't something Edward took lightly. For him, it wasn't just a matter of faith; it was a guiding force. A belief that justice, real justice, had to be rooted in something deeper, something untouchable by human hands.

Logan leaned over, placing a hand on Edward's shoulder. "You've got us, Ed. Whatever it takes, we'll follow this trail. Naudet didn't deserve what happened, and if there's someone out there pulling strings, we'll make sure they answer for it."

## Forty Seven (47)

Edward looked from Logan to Rudra, feeling the weight of their loyalty. He let out a small, grateful sigh. "I don't say this enough, but I couldn't do this without you two."

Logan chuckled, breaking the seriousness of the moment. "Good thing you don't say it often, or we'd start charging you. Friendship isn't free, you know."

Rudra's lips twitched in a rare smile. "Consider it our own mission, Edward. Just as much yours as it is ours."

With a renewed sense of determination, Edward turned back to the board, his friends at his side. Together, they would untangle the mystery of Jordan Naudet's murder — one step closer to the truth, one step closer to justice.

# The Murder Case Unfolds

47 stood before a wall of photographs, newspaper clippings, and hand-written notes. The room, dimly lit by the soft light of a desk lamp, was a far cry from the sterile professionalism of a typical detective's office. This space, rather, was a sanctuary for the unrelenting pursuit of truth. His hands moved expertly over the evidence as his sharp eyes took in every detail. The murder of Jordan Naudet was a puzzle, and he wasn't about to leave a single piece unchecked.

Naudet was a name that carried weight. He had built an empire—one that touched every corner of the globe. His company, Alliance, wasn't merely the energy business; it was a force. Jordan Naudet had carved his path to the top of the corporate world with a mix of ruthlessness and brilliance. He had a philosophy, one that captivated the minds of many: "The life you've always wanted is buried beneath everything you already have." This was more than just a quote; it was a mindset that drove him toward endless ambition. He had the resources to obtain anything, but he wanted more. He wanted control. And, ultimately, he wanted to conquer the world.

## Forty Seven (47)

Edward's mind lingered on this thought for a moment. Naudet had been a visionary, no doubt, but Edward couldn't shake the feeling that there was something more beneath the surface. Something darker. And perhaps that darkness was the reason he was now dead.

Naudet had been shot in a remote place, his life taken in a cold, calculated murder. The authorities had been baffled. No one had heard a shot, and there were no witnesses to speak of. Naudet's cat, his only companion during his final walk, was found nearby, distressed but unharmed. But that, like the murder itself, was a mystery. It didn't make sense. Someone had gone to great lengths to erase the crime, and whoever had done it was careful not to leave behind anything that could reveal their identity.

As Edward stared at the wall of evidence, one name continued to resurface: Marco Douglas. The man was a competitor, a rival, but more importantly, he was a man of considerable power in his own right. Marco Douglas had a reputation for ruthless business dealings, and from what Edward had gathered, the two men had been involved in a delicate, often adversarial, relationship. But did that rivalry extend to murder?

Edward leaned forward, his eyes narrowing as he studied the connection between Naudet and

Douglas. Their relationship was complex, built on a history of competition, alliances, and betrayals. The more Edward dug, the more he realized that there was something more to their dynamic. Douglas had been too silent in the wake of Naudet's death—too quiet for a man whose business interests had just been shaken to their core.

He pinched the bridge of his nose, trying to push aside the mounting tension in his head. It wasn't like him to jump to conclusions, but everything in him screamed that Marco Douglas was involved. The question wasn't whether Douglas had a hand in it. It was how deep his involvement went and what strings he had pulled to orchestrate Naudet's untimely demise.

With a sigh, Edward stepped away from the board, his mind still racing. He had a job to do. And for that, he needed to step outside the confines of the office and into the field. There were clues yet to uncover, and answers to be found.

Hours later, Edward, accompanied by his trusted allies, Rudradev Singh, known as Rudra, and Loganathan Singh, or Logan, stood at the edge of a dense park, the site where Jordan Naudet was last seen. The early morning light filtered through the trees, casting long shadows over the land. There was an unsettling stillness in the air, a sense of quiet that seemed out of place for such a sinister scene.

## Forty Seven (47)

The ground was damp from a recent rain, and Edward could hear the soft rustle of leaves as they moved toward the clearing.

Rudra, ever the meticulous one, crouched beside the bench, his sharp eyes scanning the area with precision. Edward could tell that Rudra's mind was already processing the scene, connecting dots in ways most would miss. He was the detail-oriented one, the one who noticed the things others overlooked. His presence was always steady, calming, like the unwavering pulse of a heart.

"There's something off here," Rudra muttered as he studied the disturbed earth around Naudet's footsteps. "Precision, but it feels rushed," he continued, his voice low. "This wasn't just a random act. Someone went to great lengths to make sure he stayed hidden."

Logan, standing a few feet away, crossed his arms and surveyed the wider scene. His ability to read people and situations was unparalleled, and it was clear he was piecing together the larger picture. Logan's mind was always a few steps ahead, processing the scenario from every angle. His intuition was a gift, and Edward trusted it implicitly.

"It's strange," Logan said, his eyes narrowing. "Naudet was powerful—he wouldn't have been caught off guard. He was too aware of his surroundings. So why is he here, unprotected? Alone?"

Edward turned his gaze toward the surroundings. The park was isolated, the trees thick enough to conceal any movements, yet it felt as though someone had intentionally chosen this spot. There were no signs of struggle, no witnesses. Whoever had done this had planned it meticulously.

"Someone wanted privacy," Edward mused, his voice steady, a deliberate calm in the face of uncertainty. "They needed time. This wasn't just a crime of passion; it was a calculated move. Whoever did this didn't want anyone to hear, didn't want anyone to question them. They wanted Naudet's death to disappear without a trace."

Logan nodded in agreement. "And he wasn't ambushed. He was brought here—maybe by someone he trusted. He didn't expect betrayal. Whoever did this knew how to deceive him."

Edward turned back to the footsteps, his mind spinning with the implications of their findings. "Which means Naudet's killer is someone he knew well. Someone close enough to gain his trust, to get him to come here without suspicion."

Rudra's voice cut through the silence. "And if we're talking about trust, that leaves us with a short list. Someone close to him—perhaps too close."

## Forty Seven (47)

Edward nodded thoughtfully. "Marco Douglas is at the top of that list."

The words hung in the air, heavy with meaning. Marco Douglas, a man who had been both a business partner and a rival, someone who knew Naudet's every move, was the person most likely to have orchestrated this murder. The question wasn't why—Naudet's power had threatened him. The real question was how. How had Douglas manipulated the situation to his advantage, and how had he convinced Naudet to walk into the trap?

After a moment of silence, Edward straightened up, his resolve hardening. "We need to go back to the office. We've gathered what we can here, but this is only the beginning."

The trio turned and walked away from the grave, each of them lost in their thoughts, processing the grim reality of what they had uncovered. They had a murderer to catch, a mastermind to unearth, and a tangled web of lies and betrayal to unravel. The path ahead would be dark and treacherous, but they were ready to confront it.

As they drove back to the office, Edward's mind raced with possibilities. Marco Douglas was a dangerous man, but he wasn't the only one who had something to gain from Naudet's death. The game was far from over, and Edward knew that the deeper he dug, the more sinister the conspiracy would become. They had only scratched the surface.

One thing was clear: Jordan Naudet had been a powerful man, and his death was no accident. Whoever had killed him had done so with intent, with purpose. And they were not done yet.

Edward Lucas, Detective 47, wasn't about to rest until he had all the answers.

# Introducing Marco Douglas and the Game of Cat and Mouse

Edward leaned back in his chair, the edges of his mouth pressed into a thin line. The lights in his office were dim, the shadows casting a mysterious, almost foreboding aura across the room. On the wall before him hung his meticulously constructed case board. It was a grim collage of faces, locations, evidence tags, and red string, each piece a fragment of the deadly puzzle he was trying to solve. And right in the center was the face that had been haunting him lately – Marco Douglas.

Marco was more than just a businessman. He was a figure of immense influence and resources, a man who'd clawed his way up the corporate ladder, accumulating both power and enemies in equal measure. His presence alone was intimidating, his reputation a cloak of danger. Marco didn't need to say much to command attention; his silence and piercing gaze often did the work. The rumors around him only added to his mystique – he was known as a man who could make people disappear, a figure of shadowy influence that went far beyond the walls of his office.

Edward's gaze lingered on the photograph he had managed to obtain of Marco Douglas, the man who had now become a central figure in this murky web of power and murder. The photo was taken at some lavish corporate event, but the intensity of Marco's presence was undeniable. He looked to be in his mid-forties, with salt-and-pepper hair slicked back with precision, a sharp jawline that seemed to carry the weight of his influence, and a demeanor that screamed control. His features were chiseled, meticulously crafted, yet there was something chilling in the way his eyes seemed to peer through the camera lens — a cold, calculating look that made Edward feel like the walls were closing in on him. There was no mistaking it: the man exuded a quiet, dangerous power. He wasn't the type to get his hands dirty in the public eye, but his influence was vast enough that he didn't need to. He was a puppeteer, and the city — no, the world — was his stage.

Edward's thoughts were interrupted by the sudden shrill ring of his phone, breaking the silence in the room like a gunshot. His body tensed instinctively, his mind already racing through the possibilities of who it could be. He glanced at the screen and saw the name that he had been expecting: Marco Douglas. His heartbeat quickened, but his

## Forty Seven (47)

expression remained unchanged. He had been waiting for this call. The game was about to change.

He took a breath, steadying himself, then answered with the calm precision of a man who had seen too many things to be easily rattled. "Detective Edward," he said, his voice unwavering.

A low chuckle came through the line, smooth and dangerous, like the sound of ice cracking in a frozen lake. "I hear you've taken an interest in me lately," Marco's voice purred, silky but with a hint of something darker lurking beneath. "Tell me, Detective... what makes you think you'll find anything that others haven't? There are dozens of people who've come before you, and none of them have gotten any closer."

Edward's grip on the phone tightened ever so slightly, the muscles in his jaw flexing, but he didn't let the tension show in his voice. His words came out slow, deliberate. "It's an occupational hazard. You come up quite frequently in my line of work."

Another chuckle echoed in the silence, this time more deliberate, as if Marco were savoring the moment. "I'm sure I do. But I must admit, I'm curious. What makes you so confident you'll succeed where everyone else has failed?"

Edward's eyes flickered to the corkboard in front of him, where Marco's photo was pinned beside a string connecting it to a photograph of Jordan

Naudet's lifeless body. The pieces were slowly falling into place, and the connections were becoming clearer. He leaned forward slightly, his voice dropping a notch, his words cutting through the air like a sharpened knife. "I suppose that's where our views differ, Mr. Douglas. Most of the people you've encountered likely had their limits. I don't."

There was a pause on the other end of the line, the kind that made the air feel thick, charged with a tension that neither man was willing to break. Marco's voice, when it returned, was colder, more calculating. "Limits," he mused, his tone almost thoughtful, as though he were considering Edward's words like a connoisseur sampling an exquisite wine. "Yes, that seems to be your kind's shortcoming, doesn't it? Lines you won't cross. Values you uphold. It's endearing... if not a little naive."

Edward's grip tightened on the phone, but he refused to let Marco's insult rattle him. His gaze hardened, and he leaned back in his chair, the creaking of the leather punctuating the silence. "Naudet's death wasn't just an unfortunate accident, Marco," he said, his voice now laced with a quiet intensity. "He was taken down with intention, with planning. Someone as meticulous as you would understand that, wouldn't they?"

## Forty Seven (47)

The silence that followed was thick, almost suffocating. Edward could feel the tension on the other end of the line as Marco absorbed his words, the atmosphere growing heavier with each passing second. The faint hum of the air conditioning in the background seemed to grow louder, underscoring the stillness. Then, Marco's voice broke through again, smoother this time, but with an edge that sent a chill down Edward's spine. "I would tread carefully if I were you, Detective. It's easy to play hero until you're faced with reality. And reality is... I have no patience for people who overstep."

The words were like a venomous threat, dripping with malice. The air in the room seemed to grow colder, the weight of Marco's unspoken power pressing down on Edward. He could almost picture the man on the other end of the line – sitting in some lavish, high-rise office, the city stretching out beneath him like a chessboard. Marco Douglas wasn't someone who made idle threats. He was someone who carried the weight of his power in every syllable, every breath. It was a warning, and it was clear: Marco wasn't afraid to eliminate anyone who stood in his way.

But Edward didn't flinch. His resolve only strengthened. He had come too far to back down now. He leaned forward again, his voice steady but full of the quiet determination that had gotten him this far. "You underestimate me, Douglas. That's a mistake I'd advise you to avoid."

For a brief moment, there was a strange quietness on the line, almost as if Marco were contemplating Edward's words. Then, his voice returned, soft but dangerously calm. "Then consider this advice in return: There are things far bigger than you, Detective. Bigger than Naudet, bigger than you can imagine. Ask yourself... if you're willing to pay the price to go up against them."

The words were like a final, ominous warning, a threat veiled in mystery. Edward felt the hairs on the back of his neck stand up, the reality of what he was up against becoming even clearer. There were forces at play here that went beyond just a murder case. The deeper he dug, the more he realized that this wasn't just about one man's death. It was about something much larger, something that had the potential to unravel everything.

Edward's grip on the phone loosened slightly, but his mind was already racing, his thoughts like a thousand gears grinding together. He had no illusions about the danger Marco posed, but he wasn't backing down. The truth had to come out, no matter the cost.

"Don't worry, Mr. Douglas," Edward said, his voice cold but resolute. "I'm just getting started."

## Forty Seven (47)

The line went dead, and Edward lowered the phone slowly, his mind already working through the next steps. The message was clear. Marco Douglas was playing a much larger game than he had anticipated. But Edward was determined to expose the truth, even if it meant going up against something far bigger than he had ever imagined.

Later that evening, Edward gathered with Rudra and Logan in his office, his close friends and allies in this perilous pursuit. They had been with him through countless cases, sharing not only the battles but the scars and victories alike. Tonight, they sat across from each other, a quiet determination in their eyes.

Rudra broke the silence first, his voice calm yet edged with the confidence that came from experience. "Marco Douglas," he said, letting the name linger in the air. "You realize the kind of enemy you're dealing with, right?"

Edward nodded. "I do. He doesn't scare me."

Logan gave a low whistle, crossing his arms as he leaned back in his chair. "You should be careful, Ed. This guy isn't like the others. He's got money, influence, a whole network of people ready to protect his interests. And if he's really involved in Naudet's murder, it's not just about catching him — it's about dismantling a fortress."

Edward glanced between his two friends, appreciating their concern but determined not to let fear dictate his decisions. "I know he's dangerous. But we're dangerous, too."

Rudra leaned forward, eyes intense. "This isn't just a power game for him, Edward. He's ruthless. People like him think they're untouchable, and they're willing to do anything to stay that way. Marco has his hands in more than we probably know — politicians, security, maybe even parts of law enforcement."

Logan's eyes narrowed thoughtfully. "People have tried to bring him down before, and none have succeeded. But I think you're onto something, Ed. If there's a way to catch him off-guard, it'll come from somewhere unexpected."

Edward held their gazes, his determination evident. "I have no illusions about the risks. Marco Douglas might be untouchable to some, but he's not untouchable to us. There's always a weakness. Always."

The room fell into silence as the weight of their task settled around them. Then Rudra spoke, his voice steady but carrying a flicker of hope. "If we're going to take him down, we'll need to be smarter than he is. We'll need more than evidence — we'll need strategy, precision, and a little bit of luck."

## Forty Seven (47)

Logan smirked, a spark of excitement lighting up his face. "Luckily, precision is what we do best. And as for luck, well... we make our own."

Rudra glanced at Edward. "Marco's used to people playing by his rules. If we want to take him down, we'll have to make him play by ours."

Edward nodded, a plan beginning to form in his mind. "Exactly. He's expecting us to come at him head-on. But we won't. We'll study him, find the cracks in his armor, and exploit them. If he wants a game, then we'll give him one he's never played before."

They shared a look, a silent understanding passing between them. This wasn't just about justice for Naudet; it was about proving that people like Marco Douglas weren't above the law. It was about showing that no matter how deep someone buried their sins, the truth could still emerge.

Rudra and Logan stood, their loyalty unwavering, their trust in Edward absolute. They were about to walk into a fight that could either bring justice to Naudet's memory or destroy them all. But they would do it together, bound by loyalty, fueled by their shared commitment to the truth.

As they exited the office, the three of them knew that the path ahead was treacherous. Yet there was no turning back. They were ready to face the storm, and with every step, they were one step closer to bringing down the man who thought himself untouchable.

---

The game of cat and mouse had officially begun.

# Edward's Inner Circle and Family Life

The day dawned with a gentle breeze wafting through the curtains, carrying with it the promise of new beginnings. Edward Lucas, immersed in the depths of his investigation, found solace in the quietude of the morning as he sat at his desk, meticulously poring over case files and notes. The weight of Jordan Naudet's disappearance bore heavily on his shoulders, each passing day bringing new challenges and uncertainties. Despite his usual intense focus, today felt different, the air tinged with a quiet anticipation he couldn't quite name.

Meanwhile, in the kitchen, Brenna bustled around, her vibrant energy infusing the space with warmth and light. Her mind, however, was preoccupied with a secret she had been harboring for weeks—a surprise she had meticulously planned and was finally ready to reveal. With a mischievous twinkle in her eye, she carefully laid out breakfast, her heart racing in sync with her excitement.

As Edward emerged from his study, his brow furrowed in concentration, Brenna greeted him with a radiant smile, barely containing her anticipation. "Good morning, my dear," she called, her voice bright and brimming with enthusiasm. "I've got a little surprise for you."

Edward, momentarily startled, looked up with a raised eyebrow. "A surprise?" he repeated, curiosity mingling with a small smile. "What's this all about?"

With a playful glint, Brenna motioned for him to sit at the table. "You'll have to wait and see," she teased, her smile widening. Edward obliged, settling into his chair and watching her with interest as she reached into the pocket of her apron, retrieving a small, intricately wrapped parcel. With a flourish, she presented it to Edward, her eyes shining.

"For me?" Edward murmured, taking the parcel with a growing sense of curiosity. He unwrapped it carefully, the layers of paper falling away to reveal a beautifully crafted wooden box. As he lifted the lid, he drew in a soft breath, captivated by the delicate pendant inside, shimmering like a constellation, each tiny star twinkling with ethereal beauty.

"It's beautiful," he whispered, his voice tinged with awe, his fingers tracing the edges of the pendant.

Brenna's eyes sparkled with a mixture of joy and nerves. She took a breath and leaned closer, her voice soft yet steady. "That's not all," she murmured, holding his gaze with an intensity that made his heart skip. "I want us to adopt a child."

The weight of her words took a moment to sink in, and then Edward's heart thudded in his chest. Adoption—a concept he had rarely thought about—suddenly felt deeply, instinctively right. He reached out, his fingers intertwining with hers, feeling the surge of their shared purpose course between them.

"Adopt a child?" he echoed softly, searching her face. "Why now? And how?"

A soft smile curved Brenna's lips. "Because love knows no bounds," she replied, her voice full of conviction. "We've wanted this for so long. We'll figure it out, together."

A wave of warmth washed over Edward. In that moment, he knew that this decision to adopt wasn't just about expanding their family—it was a way of honoring everything they had been through together. Brenna's eyes twinkled with one last bit of surprise, and she leaned in close. "My Nakshatras are good for the next two days," she confided, her excitement unmistakable. "It's the perfect time for us to bring someone into our lives."

Edward blinked, both charmed and intrigued. "Naxy what?" he repeated, unfamiliar with the concept.

Brenna chuckled softly, brushing a hand across his cheek. "They're like hidden powers in the universe. They guide us if we're willing to listen," she explained, her words gentle. "For my zodiac, these two days are auspicious for bringing new life into our home. So let's do it—let's bring our child home."

47, still puzzled, asked, "First of all, how did you even learn about this word that I can't even spell correctly?" Brenna smiled and said, "Your two Indian mates explained it to me." "Hey, we're not Indians anymore, we're Bharatiyas. So call us Bharatiyas," they chimed in. "Okay, my Bharatiya boys, please explain to your so-called sharp-minded friend what I'm talking about," Brenna said. Logan explained, "Look, mate, there are 27 constellations that influence celestial events on Earth. These 27 constellations are known as the 27 Nakshatras, and they are 300 to 400 light years apart. Based on a person's moon Nakshatra at birth, astrologers can predict powerful time periods. This is all part of Bharatiya astrology, also known as astrospeak." Eduard sighed, "Okay, my Bharatiya Interstellars, I get it."

---

The memories of their shared journey flickered through Edward's mind, each one a reminder of the resilience they had built together. There had

## Forty Seven (47)

been a balmy summer evening, years ago, when they sat together in the sterile confines of a doctor's office, anxiously awaiting news that would change their lives. "I'm sorry," the doctor had said softly. "It appears that conceiving naturally may not be an option for you."

Brenna's eyes had brimmed with tears, and Edward, feeling her pain as his own, had tightened his hold on her hand, silently vowing that they would get through this, no matter what. They had tried everything—endless tests, invasive procedures, hope followed by disappointment. "It's not fair," Brenna had whispered through her tears. "Why us?"

In the months that followed, they explored every avenue to parenthood. But through all the trials and uncertainty, one thing remained constant: the love that bound them together, unwavering and indomitable. Now, with this momentous decision to adopt, they knew they were ready.

---

Arriving at *Child Love*, the foster care organization nestled in the heart of Illinois, Edward and Brenna felt a strange blend of nerves and anticipation as they stepped through the doors. The scent of freshly baked cookies filled the air, and the walls were adorned with colorful, child-drawn artwork that added a cheerful ambiance. A friendly receptionist greeted them, her eyes twinkling with warmth as she welcomed them to the center.

"We're here to begin the adoption process," Brenna said, her voice steady despite the butterflies in her stomach. The receptionist led them down a long corridor lined with doors, each one emanating the sounds of laughter and joy, a testament to the lives touched by the love and care of this place.

Finally, they entered a cozy office where Mrs. Thompson, a gentle-faced social worker, awaited them. The room, adorned with family photos and children's drawings, felt like a comforting haven amidst the day's swirling emotions.

"Welcome, Brenna and Edward," Mrs. Thompson greeted, her warm smile settling their nerves. They exchanged introductions, and as they shared their story, Mrs. Thompson listened intently, her gaze filled with understanding and compassion. Finally, she smiled, a glimmer of excitement lighting her eyes.

"I believe we may have the perfect match for you," she announced, retrieving a file from her desk and handing it to them. Brenna and Edward held their breath as they opened it, gazing at the photograph of a bright-eyed young boy with a heart-warming smile.

"This is Joshua," Mrs. Thompson explained. "He's an energetic, curious young boy with a heart of gold." Brenna's heart swelled as she looked at the photo, feeling an immediate connection, a sense of familiarity she couldn't explain.

"He sounds perfect," she whispered, her voice laced with emotion. "We'd love to meet him."

With Mrs. Thompson's guidance, they walked down another corridor until they reached a cozy playroom. There, a young boy sat cross-legged on the floor, engrossed in a puzzle. Mrs. Thompson gently called his name, and the boy looked up, his gaze falling on Brenna and Edward.

At first, he seemed shy, glancing between them and Mrs. Thompson with uncertainty. But then, as if sensing the love and kindness emanating from them, a tentative smile spread across his face. "Hi," he said softly.

Brenna felt her heart melt. She and Edward stepped closer, their movements gentle, their voices soft. "Hello, Joshua," she said, kneeling down to his level. "My name is Brenna, and this is my husband, Edward. We've been so excited to meet you." Edward personally met the child, Josh, and introduced himself, "I'm Edward Lucas. Do you like the name Lucas?" Josh asked, "Why?" Edward explained, "It means 'bringer of light.' It's a name for someone who will bring light into their family's life. Would you like to be called Josh Lucas?" Josh smiled and replied, "Yeah, sure, Edward." Edward corrected him, "Hey, don't call me by my name. I'm your father now—call me Dad." "Okay, Dad," Josh responded.

Joshua's eyes sparkled as he studied them, and Brenna joined Edward, crouching beside him. They began talking, about his favorite games, his love for puzzles, and the stories he adored. In the warmth of the playroom, with laughter and quiet conversation weaving through the space, a bond was forged—a promise of love and acceptance.

They spent the rest of the afternoon with Joshua, talking, laughing, and slowly easing his apprehension. Each passing moment deepened their certainty, filling them with a joy they had almost forgotten was possible. As the sun dipped below the horizon, painting the sky in hues of pink and orange, they knew in their hearts that their family was complete.

# The First Major Clue – The Protruding Finger

While Brenna was talking to Josh, a strange man approached Eduard. "Mr. 47, I need to speak with you," the man said. "How do you know my name?" Eduard asked, surprised. "You're a famous detective—who hasn't heard of you?" the stranger replied. "Besides that, I wanted to tell you that while I was traveling in Minnetonka in a taxi, I saw something strange. A finger was protruding from a trash bag under the seat where I was sitting, as the trunk of the taxi was damaged. I thought this might be relevant to the case of Jordan Naudet, who has been missing since that day."

"You're suggesting that Mr. Naudet was murdered?" Eduard asked. "I'm not sure, sir, but I thought you should know about this," the stranger said. "What's your name?" Eduard inquired. "My name is Andrew Davis, sir," the man replied. "Thank you, Mr. Davis. This information could be crucial to my case," Eduard said. "Do you have any details about the taxi or the driver?" "I can recognize the driver if I see him again, and the taxi's number was 5849," Davis replied. "Can you give me your contact information?" Eduard asked. "Sure," Davis said, handing over his card before leaving.

Eduard re-joined Brenna and Josh. "Where were you?" Brenna asked. "I think our son has already brought some light to this case, even before coming home," Eduard said. "What do you mean?" Brenna asked. "Nothing, just talking to a stranger," Eduard replied. "Alright, let's head back to Minnetonka," Brenna said.

They arrived at Eduard's flat, and Josh met 47's two mates. Brenna introduced them, "This is Rudra, the elder one, and Logan, the younger one." "Logan, like Wolverine?" Josh asked. "No, that's just a nickname," Logan laughed. "My full name is Loganathan Singh, and his name is Rudradev Singh. We're Bharatiyas, not Indians, as our country is going to be renamed Bharat, like it was called Bharatvarsha." "You must be tired from the trip. Get some rest, and we'll meet in the morning," they suggested.

The next morning, 47 turned on the TV and started watching Areus News Channel. The first segment was a health bulletin, including the Humanitarian Response Plan of the USA. Next was a missing persons bulletin for Jordan Naudet, followed by updates on real estate, work requirements, and financial bulletins. The final segment was a marketing bulletin about Marcus Douglas's rise

## Forty Seven (47)

from near bankruptcy, noting that while Douglas had moved up the list of the world's wealthiest men, he was still far behind Naudet.

Rudra joined 47 and asked, "What's the update on the Naudet case?" "We're making progress, moving closer to solving it," 47 replied. "How do you feel about it?" Rudra asked. "We may encounter many setbacks, but we're not defeated yet," 47 responded. "Failure is part of success, not its opposite. And I think we've found a crucial lead in this case." "What are you talking about, and when did this happen?" Rudra asked, surprised. "I think it's my son who brought hope to this case," 47 said. "What! How?" Rudra asked. "Yesterday, in Illinois, I met a stranger named Andrew Davis. He mentioned seeing a finger protruding from a taxi in Minnetonka. I think it might be Naudet," 47 explained. "And you think it's Naudet?" Rudra asked. "I'm not sure, but we should approach this evidence with a thorough and analytical response. As we know, curiosity is the opportunity to bring our best and make the biggest difference," 47 concluded.

Eduard said, "I've got the taxi number, and the stranger, Davis, is certain he can identify the driver. We should inquire with the local people near the park where Naudet was last seen and also involve the local authorities since they're better positioned to respond to this missing person case. It's important to consider the views of the public, as it has a strong psychological impact. If necessary, involve others—call, consult, push the investigation forward. Be sure to inform your brother as well," Eduard instructed Rudra.

Just then, Josh appeared out of nowhere, having overheard the word "respond." Curious as always, he asked, "What does that word mean?" Logan, who had joined them, explained, "The word 'respond' basically means to show or have a good or quick reaction, like I'm doing now by answering your question. It's like how we respond to a demand—just like how health care, government benefits, distance learning, work, digital services, groceries, and online shopping all responded strongly during COVID-19." "Okay, I got it, Uncle Logan," Josh said with a smile.

"Alright, back to work," said 47. Rudra asked, "Will the local public help us with information?" "Yes, we have a right to information and the obligation of the public and public authorities to assist. We should consider this case extensively. Those who work extensively every day, testing how things are clarified by their knowledge, tend to become faultless in their approach," Eduard responded. He then instructed the two brothers to compare intensive and extensive matters.

The next day was the United States presidential inauguration. The president-elect was about to be

## Forty Seven (47)

sworn in by taking the presidential oath of office. The weather was cold, and the city was bustling with crowds, traffic, and other logistical challenges as citizens showed their support.

Edward Lucas had spent countless hours reviewing case files, analyzing every small piece of evidence in his pursuit of Jordan Naudet, the missing energy mogul whose sudden disappearance had rocked the city. The investigation had taken twists and turns, but nothing had led him any closer to finding Naudet or determining whether foul play was involved. The more he dug, the deeper the trail seemed to disappear, and with each passing day, his frustration grew.

The ringing of his phone broke the silence in the dim-lit office. Edward's hand instinctively moved to answer it, his mind still caught up in the complex web of possibilities surrounding Naudet's disappearance.

"Lucas," he said, his voice steady but with an underlying edge of weariness.

"Detective Lucas, this is Officer Martinez. We've found something you need to see," the voice on the other end crackled, a note of urgency creeping in.

Edward's pulse quickened. He straightened in his chair. "What is it? What's happened?"

"It's... it's a finger. We found a finger sticking out of a trash bag behind a diner off Fifth Street. It's fresh, and we're sending it to the lab. But you should come down here immediately. Something doesn't sit right."

"A finger?" Edward repeated, the words sinking in. His mind raced. A clue this significant couldn't be a coincidence. Edward thought he recently got a protruding finger lead and now this call. This could be the break he had been waiting for. Or this may be a trap to avoid suspicion.

"I'm on my way," Edward replied, already reaching for his jacket and car keys.

The drive to Fifth Street felt like an eternity. The dark sky and empty streets only served to amplify Edward's sense of urgency. What did the finger mean? Was this the first real sign of a body? Was it Naudet's? The questions rattled around in his mind, drowning out the sound of tires skimming across the rain-slick pavement.

When he arrived at the scene, a small crowd of officers and investigators had already gathered. Officer Martinez was standing by a marked evidence tent, a look of discomfort on his face as he approached Edward.

"You found it?" Edward asked, his voice low and steady, though his heart was pounding in his chest.

## Forty Seven (47)

Martinez nodded grimly. "Yeah. Right in that trash bag. We've secured the area, but we're waiting for the forensics team to give us the go-ahead. The strangest thing is how it was placed. Just the finger, sticking out like it was... meant to be found."

Edward didn't wait for further explanation. He ducked under the tent and approached the bag that had caught their attention. Inside, a single finger jutted out from a tangle of refuse. The severed digit was unmistakable, and its freshness left no doubt—it had been removed recently. The rest of the body was nowhere to be seen.

As he stared at the gruesome sight, a thought gnawed at him. It wasn't just the finger that was strange—it was the way it had been discarded. It was almost as if someone wanted it to find it. But why? And why only a finger?

He looked over at Martinez, who seemed just as perplexed. "We need to pull the CCTV footage from around here," Edward said firmly. "I want to see who dumped this. Now."

Martinez immediately set the wheels in motion, radioing the team to begin reviewing the cameras from the area.

Back at the precinct, Edward and his team gathered in a small, dimly lit room. The large screen on the wall flickered to life, showing a grainy image of a busy street corner. Logan, a seasoned investigator with a keen eye for details, squinted at the footage. Beside him, Rudra, a tech expert with a penchant for spotting irregularities, was quickly tapping at the keyboard, pulling up footage from various angles. Edward stood behind them, tension building in his chest.

The first few minutes of footage were uneventful. Pedestrians walked by, unaware of the sinister events unfolding in their midst. Then, at precisely 2:34 AM, a taxi pulled into view. The vehicle slowed as it approached a corner, stopping near the dumpster where the trash bags had been left. Edward's gaze sharpened. The driver emerged, and, though the footage was grainy, Edward could make out the shape of several heavy bags in the driver's hands.

"That's odd," Logan murmured, his voice low. "That driver's not just handling one bag—he's handling a few. And that's not typical for someone dropping off trash."

Edward nodded. "You're right. It looks like he's trying to get rid of something, but why so many bags?"

Rudra leaned in, zooming in on the footage. "Wait. Look at the way he's handling those bags. They're bulky, but he's being careful with them. It's almost like he doesn't want them to fall apart."

## Forty Seven (47)

"Let's see where he goes," Edward said, his focus unwavering. He was already piecing together the puzzle in his mind.

Rudra worked the controls, pulling up the route taken by the taxi. "I've got it," he said after a few moments. "The taxi took a right on Fifth, then another left down Main, and eventually... headed out of the city. It's heading towards Minnetonka's forests."

Edward's heart skipped a beat. Minnetonka. The name rang a bell. That was the area where Naudet had been last seen. His team had scoured the place for any sign of him, but there had been no luck. If this driver was headed in that direction, it might be the lead they needed.

"Logan, Rudra—track down this driver. We need to find out who he is and where he went. And if this guy has any connection to Naudet, I want to know immediately," Edward ordered, his voice taut with urgency.

---

Hours later, the team had managed to identify the taxi driver. His name was Michael James, and he had a lengthy criminal record. The deeper they dug, the more they uncovered. James had been involved in low-level smuggling operations in the past. The more Edward thought about it, the more he was convinced that James wasn't just some random driver. There was something about his careful handling of the trash bags, the fact that he was heading toward Minnetonka—it all pointed to something more sinister.

They tracked down James's last known location, and a team of officers was dispatched to interrogate him. As the minutes ticked by, Edward couldn't shake the nagging feeling that they were on the cusp of something big. They were getting closer to finding Naudet, or at least discovering what had happened to him.

At the same time, Logan and Rudra were making connections of their own. Logan's keen instincts had noticed something strange in the footage: the way James had parked the taxi. It wasn't in a public space, but rather tucked away behind an old, unused warehouse just outside the city.

Rudra, meanwhile, had pulled up financial records for the taxi service and uncovered a suspicious payment made just days before Naudet's disappearance. The payment came from a shell company with ties to an offshore account—a connection to Naudet's business empire that could no longer be ignored.

"Everything's pointing to Minnetonka," Logan said, his voice tight with resolve. "We've got to move fast."

## Forty Seven (47)

Edward agreed. "Let's go," he said, turning toward the door. "It's time to find out what happened to Jordan Naudet. I don't think we're going to like what we find, but we need to know."

Minnetonka was just a short drive away, but as Edward's car cruised through the quiet streets, the weight of the moment pressed down on him. They were getting close. The finger—the taxi driver—the strange route—it all led here, to this unassuming town. Whatever they uncovered next could change everything.

As they approached the area where James had parked the taxi, Edward felt a twinge of unease. The street was empty, the buildings silent in the moonlight. It was too quiet. But then, there it was—the warehouse. The very same one James had parked behind in the footage.

He motioned for the team to spread out. They approached the building cautiously, moving in the shadows, knowing that whatever lay inside could be the key to unraveling the mystery of Naudet's disappearance.

# Close Call and Rising Tensions

The moonlight glinted off the rain-soaked streets as Edward and his team approached the old warehouse. Every instinct in Edward's gut screamed that they were closing in on something monumental—something dangerous. The night had grown eerily quiet, with only the soft sound of footsteps and the occasional crackle of their radios breaking the silence.

They had found the location where the taxi driver had made his unusual stop. Now, they were about to confront Michael James—the driver who, as it turned out, had been more involved in the case than anyone had anticipated. The pieces of the puzzle were slowly falling into place, but Edward could feel the tension in the air. Something didn't feel right.

"Stay sharp," Edward murmured to Logan and Rudra, who flanked him as they moved toward the warehouse's main entrance. The building was old, industrial, and seemingly abandoned, but Edward wasn't fooled. There was something hidden here—

## Forty Seven (47)

something far more dangerous than any of them had expected.

They crept up to a side door, the only way in. It was slightly ajar, the faintest hint of light spilling out from the crack. Edward motioned for them to be silent, and with one swift motion, he pushed the door open. The creaking sound of the hinges echoed through the empty space, sending a shiver down his spine.

Inside, the warehouse was dark, save for a few dim lights scattered across the floor. They could barely make out the figures of crates and metal structures looming in the shadows. But they could hear something: soft, irregular breathing.

Michael James was sitting against one of the crates, his hands tied behind his back, his face pale and nervous. He looked up as Edward and his team stepped into the room. The fear in his eyes was undeniable.

"James," Edward said, his voice steady but firm. "You're not in any trouble. Just tell us what happened. Why were you dumping those trash bags? What did you see?"

The driver swallowed hard, his voice trembling as he spoke. "I didn't want to do it. I swear to you, I didn't. But... he made me. He had a gun, and he told me not to ask any questions. He said if I didn't do exactly what he told me, I wouldn't make it out of here alive. I... I don't know who he was. I didn't see his face, but he was tall, wearing a mask... and he was fast. He said he'd been watching me for days."

Edward's jaw clenched. The urgency of James's words sent a chill through him. A masked man with a gun. Someone powerful enough to coerce a taxi driver into doing their bidding. Edward's suspicions were growing stronger. He wasn't dealing with just a petty criminal here; this was something much bigger. Someone wanted to keep them from finding out the truth.

"Where did he go?" Logan asked, his voice sharp. "What did he say?"

James shook his head, looking panicked. "I don't know where he went. He made me drop the bags, and then he told me to leave. He didn't even give me a chance to ask questions, just shoved me in the car and told me to drive away. I don't know where he went after that."

Edward stepped closer, trying to keep his tone calm. "What did he look like? Anything that could help us track him down?"

James wiped his face with the back of his hand. "All I saw was his eyes. He had these cold, empty eyes... like he didn't care about anything. And the voice— deep, like it was muffled through a filter. He said... he said I better keep my mouth shut or else."

## Forty Seven (47)

The lack of details made Edward's gut twist. Whoever this man was, he wasn't just a hired gun—he was part of something much more sinister, something Edward was now tangled up in. The pieces of the case were starting to come together, but they were painting a picture Edward wasn't sure he wanted to see.

"You've done the right thing by telling us what you know," Edward said, trying to reassure James, though his mind was already racing with thoughts of what to do next. "You're going to be okay. Just sit tight, we'll get you out of here."

As they untied James and prepared to leave the warehouse, Edward couldn't shake the feeling that they were walking into a trap. Someone didn't want them getting too close to the truth—and that someone had the power to make sure they didn't.

---

The next day, Edward sat in his office, staring at the evidence that had been piling up over the past few days. It was clear that they were getting closer to something far larger than a missing person case. But every time they uncovered a new lead, it only seemed to deepen the mystery.

He picked up his phone, checking for any updates from Logan and Rudra. He hadn't heard back from them yet, but he knew they were working on tracing James's claims about the mysterious man. The warehouse, too, had yielded little—no fingerprints, no signs of a struggle, and no further clues about the man who had coerced James.

As he leaned back in his chair, his phone buzzed. It was an unknown number. Edward didn't hesitate to answer it.

"Detective Lucas," he said, his voice steady.

"Well, well, Detective Lucas, you're getting closer, aren't you?" The voice on the other end was low, almost taunting. It was calm, controlled, but there was a clear thread of amusement running through it. Edward's skin prickled.

"Who is this?" Edward demanded, a surge of adrenaline rushing through him.

"I think you know who this is," the voice replied. "You've been poking around a little too much, Lucas. I have to admit, I'm impressed. But if you think you're going to walk out of this unscathed, you're wrong. You should be careful—there's a lot at stake here. Things you don't understand. You might want to stop digging before you go too deep."

Edward's jaw tightened. "What do you want?"

The voice chuckled darkly. "I don't want anything. But you're getting dangerously close to something I don't think you're ready for. You'd better think long and hard about how far you're willing to go.

## Forty Seven (47)

You don't know who you're dealing with, Detective."

The call abruptly ended, and Edward was left with nothing but the cold silence of the room. His heart was racing. He had suspected something was off, but this was confirmation—someone powerful, someone dangerous, was pulling the strings behind the scenes. And now, they were warning him to back off.

Edward stood up, his hands clenched into fists. He was no stranger to danger, but the stakes had never been this high. This wasn't just a missing person anymore. This was a game of power, and he had just been drawn into the middle of it.

His phone buzzed again, snapping him out of his thoughts. It was Logan.

"Boss, we found something," Logan's voice crackled through the line. "We've traced the shell company back to a powerful corporation in the energy sector. And guess who's behind it?"

Edward's heart sank. "Tell me."

"It's Marco Douglas. He's the one pulling the strings, Lucas."

Edward's stomach churned. Marco Douglas—an influential player in the city's energy market. A man with the kind of power and resources to make Edward's investigation disappear in an instant.

And now, Marco knew they were on his trail.

"Keep digging," Edward said, his voice hardening with resolve. "I'm not backing down. Let's get him."

But deep down, Edward knew that confronting Marco would take him to dangerous heights. They were treading on thin ice now. One wrong move, and they could all be swallowed up by the darkness of forces they weren't prepared to face.

# Love Romance & Relationship

Back at the flat, Eduard was staring at Brenna. "Is there a reason you're staring at me?" Brenna asked. "I'm not staring at you; I'm just lost in thought," Eduard teased. "Shut up, Eduard. I know that look," Brenna replied, smiling. He continued gazing into her eyes—bronze, brown, and full of warmth. The intensity of his gaze was unlike anything she'd experienced before, as if she was the center of his universe, his whole world. Overcome with shyness, she wanted to look away, but he wouldn't let her. The connection between them was burning bright, like a fire kindling slowly and then erupting into an all-consuming blaze.

Their chemistry began with mild warmth, then intensified from medium to hot, until it felt like they were burning at the very core of their beings. In their youth, they had always been passionate, and now, as adults, that fire only grew stronger. They communicated on a deep, gut level, sharing a secret moment of vulnerability and connection.

Afterward, they talked, sharing ideas and judgments, and learning new things about each other. What began as intense passion ended in a cliché but comforting conversation, leaving them both feeling like blank sheets of paper, ready to rethink their lives together. They switched on the TV.

Anna Thomas, the well-known correspondent of Areus News, was live with a business report. She discussed financial companies and the importance of providing necessary information in financial statements so that users who can read them are better positioned to make important decisions. While watching, Brenna turned to Eduard and said, "We should have a proper home now. We're a family—you're a father, and we have a son. It's time to build our own home."

"Okay, we'll build our home. Do you have any ideas?" Eduard asked. "My family is well settled in California," Brenna said. "We could build our dream home there. I've already thought about the construction and design. We'll contact the local builder who built my family home. He can also help us lease land from a local farmer and arrange for plumbing, electrical work, and lighting. We'll need to think about space planning, environmental health, safety, sanitation, and grounds keeping too."

Eduard's two mates returned to the flat after visiting the park and Naudet's home, as they were tasked with gathering information from the locals.

## Forty Seven (47)

They noticed something strange about Naudet's pet cat and reported it to 47. "What did you find?" 47 asked. "The cat kept staring at the crucifix as if it was trying to communicate something," they said. "Naudet's family mentioned that the cat was with him when he went to the park that evening."

47 remarked, "An animal is usually referred to as 'it' unless the relationship is personal, like with Naudet's pet. There are countless procedures carried out on common pets in research, but they provide us with special companionship. Animals are intelligent and faithful; we need to figure out what this cat is trying to tell us." "The cat is playing with the cross using its mouth and paw," Logan added.

Meanwhile, Anna was back on Areus News with a segment on Douglas's financial moves. "Douglas has made his first scoring shot by becoming a foreign portfolio investor. He's bought financial assets in China, including fixed deposits and mutual funds, positioning himself as a significant player in the global market," Eduard noted, watching the news. "This move will strengthen his empire significantly, as he's invested in housing finance companies, microfinance institutions, and real estate. He's also focused on supporting employers and employees, marking this as a 'force majeure' initiative."

The next news was about Firm Alliance. The board members had launched a 20 lakh crore economic stimulus package after consulting with every section of the company, aiming to make the company self-reliant after the major setback of Naudet's disappearance. ACE founder Marcus Douglas's stake had risen as his company grew faster, and he had also invested heavily in print media and outdoor promotions.

But Jordan Naudet's thinking was on a larger scale. He applied a simple formula to his company: "Never let a win go to your head or a loss to your heart. Trading is a game of probabilities. You don't have to be right every time; you just have to follow your instinct." He had advised his employees, "Do not risk more than 1-2% of your capital per trade. A trader seeks consistent performance, but a gambler looks for quick profit." These ideas and principles were outlined in his book, Trading Capital.

Naudet had an optimal capital structure and implemented growth initiatives that kept his company afloat even after his disappearance. He balanced leverage and deleverage strategies, upgraded credit ratings, and ensured access to capital markets. He also advised his employees to preserve cash and working capital, using rapid procurement levers to support finances during

## Forty Seven (47)

crises. Trading Capital contained many of these economic insights.

Brenna entered the room, holding a rose. "For you, my love," she said to Eduard. "You're so important to me. I wanted to take the time to tell you how special you are."

"Oh, thank you, my love," Eduard replied. "Our love makes ordinary moments extraordinary. Now, please remove your jewellery. Our work is about to commence."

"What work?" Brenna asked.

"This is our time for commencing our private proceedings," Eduard said with a playful grin. "Shut down all your work; this person will now destroy you," Eduard added, excitedly.

"You boys are all the same," Brenna teased.

"Yeah, we're different, we're the same, and we're marvelous," Eduard said. "Now, let's go to war."

"Okay," Brenna agreed with a smile.

Later, Eduard and Brenna sat under the clear sky. Brenna said, "No matter how far apart we are, we will always be under the same sky."

"My answer is the same—nothing much changes," Eduard replied.

"Shut up, Eduard," Brenna laughed.

"Okay, sorry. Yeah, we're all aspects of one great being. No matter how far apart we are, the air connects us. We'll never be alone," Eduard reassured her. "In this life, we'll never truly be apart. We'll live our lives to the same beat of our hearts. We'll play our roles, side by side or miles apart."

"Yes, my love, we'll share pieces of ourselves and hustle through life together. We are chosen by God. We'll discover new voices and engage in fresh conversations. We'll converge and rebalance together," Brenna said, full of hope.

"What about our kid, Josh?" Brenna asked Eduard.

Eduard replied, "I've always been a good kid and want the same for my son. As someone who's grown up interacting with people from all backgrounds, cultures, and nationalities, I want to raise Josh with the same abilities. I plan to keep him engaged with a variety of activities. I see him as someone who enjoys exploring different things, and I believe that with effort, I can cultivate his interests in various fields. I'll focus on his passions and integrate them into his education. I want him to be a good team player, easy going, and understanding. I'll encourage him to work in groups with his friends, foster his eagerness to learn, and help him succeed in simple projects. I believe he has the potential to create something significant and make a real difference."

## Forty Seven (47)

"What are your views on our kid?" Eduard asked Brenna.

Brenna responded, "I value structure and analysis. I'll teach Josh to appreciate problem-solving and relate it to his life experiences. This approach will encourage him to consider careers where his strengths can shine. I'll ensure that his skills and interests fit together harmoniously, creating a well-rounded picture of beauty and structure. I also want him to understand society and sociology. I hope to keep up with the latest scientific breakthroughs and integrate them into his education. But right now, we should focus on the basics. He's only eleven years old. We should consider his schooling and nurture his development with activities like colors, counting, first words, bath time, water play, and toys. These will help develop his sensory and fine motor skills."

# Anna Thomas and Cathy Ron Join the Team

The morning air was crisp as Edward stood by his office window, staring out at the cityscape. The rising sun bathed the skyline in hues of gold and orange, but there was no warmth in his thoughts. The investigation was at a standstill, and the weight of the case pressed heavily on his shoulders. Naudet's disappearance had unravelled too many threads, leading to too many questions without clear answers. The deeper Edward dug, the more elusive the truth became. He needed help. And the phone call he'd received that morning had promised exactly that.

"Mr. Lucas, you have visitors," his assistant's voice broke through the silence, a hint of urgency in her tone.

Edward straightened his posture. He had been expecting Anna Thomas, a well-known figure in the world of investigative journalism. It was time to bring her in.

As he made his way to the conference room, he couldn't help but feel a mixture of anticipation and skepticism. Anna was accomplished in her own

## Forty Seven (47)

right, but the investigation had already taken so many unexpected turns that he wasn't sure how much help they could be. Still, he needed fresh eyes on the case.

The door to the conference room opened, and Anna Thomas walked in. She was tall, with sharp, intelligent eyes and a purposeful stride that made her presence impossible to ignore. Her reputation as a no-nonsense investigative reporter was well-known, and Edward had heard stories about her relentless pursuit of the truth, even if it meant going against powerful figures.

"Edward," she said, offering a brief but firm handshake. "I've read the reports. You're in the middle of something big here."

Edward nodded, trying not to let the slight tension in his chest show. There was something about Anna's directness that both intrigued and unnerved him. They had crossed paths a few times before—at press conferences, public forums, and the like—but this was the first time they were working together. There was a strange energy in the room, a subtle tension that Edward couldn't quite place.

"Welcome aboard," Edward replied, motioning to the seats around the table. "We could definitely use your expertise."

Anna nodded as she took a seat, her sharp gaze never leaving Edward's face. There was an unreadable quality to her expression, as if she was assessing him in the same way she assessed every lead she followed. But there was something else there too—a flicker of familiarity that Edward couldn't shake.

Before he could dwell on it further, the door opened again, and Cathy Ron entered the room. Unlike Anna, Cathy had a more laid-back demeanor, but that didn't mean she wasn't sharp. In fact, her calm and analytical approach to solving problems had earned her a reputation as one of the best in the field. She was Anna's former colleague, and together they made an impressive team.

"Edward," Cathy said with a friendly grin, her tone casual but confident. "I've heard a lot about this case. Let's get to work, shall we?"

Edward nodded and gestured for her to sit as well. Cathy's presence was a welcome contrast to Anna's intensity, but that didn't mean she was any less competent. They would balance each other out, he thought. The mix of their styles—Anna's bold, investigative nature and Cathy's more methodical approach—was exactly what the team needed.

"We're glad to have you both here," Edward said, settling into his seat. "We've hit a few walls recently, and I could use some fresh perspectives. Let's dive into what we know so far."

## Forty Seven (47)

As they began discussing the details of the case, Edward found himself both impressed and slightly unsettled by Anna's quick grasp of the situation. She was already asking questions that Edward hadn't considered, offering angles that were both practical and, at times, startlingly insightful. Cathy, too, seemed to have a natural gift for uncovering patterns in seemingly random data. The two of them made a formidable pair, and Edward couldn't help but feel a sense of relief that he'd brought them in.

As the hours passed, the team worked through evidence and potential leads, brainstorming and dissecting each possibility. Despite the mounting pressure of the case, Edward couldn't ignore the growing tension between him and Anna. She was focused, determined, but there was something in her eyes—a flicker of recognition or perhaps something else—that kept drawing his attention. It was as if they had a connection that neither of them had fully acknowledged.

The phone on Edward's desk buzzed, breaking the silence that had settled over the room. It was his assistant again. "Mr. Lucas, Joshua's here," she said, sounding slightly hesitant.

Edward's heart gave a small lurch at the mention of his son. He hadn't planned to have Joshua in the office today, but the boy had been insistent, wanting to see his father and maybe offer some distractions from the tense atmosphere that had been weighing down the house lately.

"Send him in," Edward said, his voice softer than he intended. He could hear Anna and Cathy's murmurs in the background, but his focus was on the door.

A few moments later, the door opened again, and Joshua walked in, his small frame barely visible behind a stack of papers he was carrying. He was only eleven, but already he had an inquisitive mind that matched Edward's own. His dark brown eyes sparkled with curiosity as he looked around the room.

"Hey, Dad," Joshua said, his voice light but filled with that familiar energy Edward had come to love. "I brought you some notes I made while reading through the case files."

Edward chuckled, feeling a sense of warmth spread through him despite the tension. "Thanks, buddy," he said, ruffling his son's hair. "I'm glad you're helping out."

Joshua's enthusiasm was contagious. As the investigation swirled around them, Joshua's innocent curiosity reminded Edward of the simple joy of solving problems, of piecing together puzzles. It brought a touch of lightness to the otherwise heavy atmosphere in the room.

## Forty Seven (47)

Anna glanced over at the young boy and raised an eyebrow. "Your son?" she asked, her voice neutral but curious.

"Yeah," Edward said, his expression softening as he looked at Joshua. "He's been helping me with some of the case work. He's got a good eye for details."

Cathy leaned back in his chair, a smile tugging at the corner of her mouth. "Looks like you've got a future investigator on your hands."

Joshua beamed at the compliment, clearly pleased. He handed Edward the papers he'd been carrying, which were covered in his neat handwriting. Edward took the notes, quickly scanning through them.

"These are great, Joshua. Thanks," Edward said, feeling a rush of pride.

As the meeting continued, Joshua's presence became a grounding force, offering Edward brief moments of respite from the growing tension surrounding the case. While Anna and Cathy worked through the details of the investigation, Edward found himself reflecting on the past few years, on the decision to adopt Joshua and bring him into his life. It had been a difficult choice, but one he didn't regret.

Despite the darkness of the investigation, Joshua's curiosity reminded Edward that there was still hope, still the possibility of understanding and truth. It was a small, personal moment in the middle of the chaos, but it was enough to remind Edward of what he was fighting for.

As the day wore on, the team made progress, but Edward couldn't shake the feeling that something much larger was at play. The connection between Naudet's disappearance and the shadowy forces behind it was becoming more apparent, and with Anna and Cathy on board, he felt they were closer than ever to uncovering the truth.

But as the sun began to set, Edward knew one thing for certain: The investigation was about to take a darker turn, and the stakes were higher than ever.

# Edward's Growing Bond with Joshua

The evening sky was painted in deep shades of purple and gold, the kind of twilight that made everything seem a little softer, a little more manageable. Edward stood in the kitchen, his back turned as he stirred the contents of a pot on the stove. The house was quiet, save for the sound of boiling water and the soft hum of the refrigerator. Joshua had come home earlier than usual today, having spent the afternoon running errands with his schoolmates. Despite the chaotic, often dangerous nature of the investigation, Edward had been trying to keep his evenings as normal as possible for Joshua. After all, the last thing the boy needed was to feel the weight of the world on his shoulders.

"Smells good," Joshua said, his voice light and unburdened by the heaviness that seemed to constantly surround Edward lately. He entered the kitchen, carrying a small bag of groceries in his hands.

"Hey, buddy," Edward said, offering a smile that was both warm and tired. "Good day?"

Joshua nodded, placing the bag on the counter. "Yeah, we did some research for school. I finished early and thought I'd come home to help."

Edward looked at his son, the way his eyes were still bright with youthful curiosity. Joshua's presence always seemed to provide a sense of calm in Edward's otherwise chaotic world. It was hard not to appreciate the boy's unassuming nature. There was something about his curiosity—his genuine desire to learn—that made Edward forget, for a brief moment, about the mounting tension in his work.

"How about we make dinner together?" Edward suggested, trying to keep the atmosphere light. "You can teach me what you've learned today."

Joshua's face lit up with excitement, his eyes sparkling as he grabbed an apron from the drawer. "I'm not a chef, but I can definitely help you with the basics."

As they prepared dinner together, Edward found himself drifting between the present moment and memories from his past. His mind wandered back to a time when he was much younger, when his own father had taught him how to cook in their small, cluttered kitchen. Those had been simpler days, before the weight of responsibility had consumed him, before the cases, the darkness, and the secrets had clouded his vision. His father had been strict but loving, a man whose protective

## Forty Seven (47)

instincts had never faltered, even when the world around them had been falling apart.

Edward had always admired his father for his ability to stay calm, to provide for the family, even when things seemed uncertain. But somewhere along the way, that sense of security had been broken. Edward had been left to pick up the pieces, to build his own sense of stability. And when Joshua came into his life, he had made a promise to himself—to be the kind of father his own had been, the kind of man who would always be there for his son, no matter what.

But the case that had landed him here—Naudet's disappearance—was threatening everything. It was as if the closer Edward got to the truth, the more dangerous things became. He couldn't allow his personal feelings to cloud his judgment. Yet, as he looked at Joshua, he felt a fierce protective instinct rising inside him. His son's innocence, his youth, was something Edward would do anything to preserve. The last thing he doesn't wanted was for Joshua to be caught up in the dangers of this investigation.

"Dad?" Joshua's voice broke through his thoughts.

Edward blinked, looking up to find Joshua standing at the counter, his brows furrowed in concern. "You alright?"

"Yeah, I'm fine," Edward replied quickly, shaking off the weight of his memories. "Just thinking."

"About the case?" Joshua asked, his tone soft yet perceptive. Edward had never been one to hide things from Joshua, but he also didn't want to burden him with the danger that loomed over them both.

"I've been thinking about a lot of things," Edward said, his voice taking on a gentle, almost nostalgic tone. "How I can keep you safe. How to make sure you don't get dragged into something dangerous."

Joshua tilted his head slightly, a thoughtful look on his face. "I know you're working on something big, but I can handle it, Dad. I'm not a little kid anymore."

Edward chuckled, though it was more out of nervousness than amusement. "I know. But you're still my responsibility, you know that?"

Joshua smiled, his youthful optimism shining through. "You don't have to worry about me, Dad. I've got you."

The warmth of the moment lasted only a few seconds before the doorbell rang, breaking the bubble of domesticity. Joshua turned toward the door, his curiosity piqued, but Edward was already heading toward it, his protective instincts flaring. The timing of the visit wasn't lost on him; in his

## Forty Seven (47)

line of work, unexpected visitors rarely meant anything good.

Edward opened the door to find Anna Thomas standing in the hallway, her hands tucked in the pockets of her jacket. She wasn't alone—Cathy Ron was with her, her expression calm but intense, a sign that she had found something worth discussing.

"Evening, Edward," Anna greeted him, her voice steady, though there was an edge to it. "We need to talk."

"Of course," Edward said, stepping aside to let them in. Joshua, sensing the change in the atmosphere, retreated into the living room, casting a curious glance over his shoulder. Edward didn't want to involve him in the conversation, but he knew his son was perceptive enough to pick up on the shift.

"Got a lead?" Edward asked as he closed the door behind them.

Anna nodded, her face serious. "It's more than that. We've uncovered something that connects Naudet's disappearance to a larger conspiracy. There are pieces of evidence that point to someone much bigger pulling the strings behind the scenes."

Edward's heart quickened at the mention of a conspiracy. He had suspected that this case was never just about Naudet, but to hear it confirmed in such a direct way was unsettling. The stakes were rising, and with them, the danger to everyone involved.

"What are we looking at?" Edward asked, his tone now all business.

Cathy pulled out a folder from her bag, flipping it open to reveal a series of documents and photographs. "We found connections between Naudet's company and several high-profile politicians, as well as ties to organized crime. It looks like Naudet might have been trying to cut off some dangerous people, and that's what got him killed."

Edward scanned the documents quickly, his mind racing. "How did Naudet get mixed up in all of this?"

"That's what we're still trying to figure out," Anna replied. "But it's clear that the people behind this aren't afraid to eliminate anyone who stands in their way."

Edward felt a knot tighten in his stomach. The investigation was no longer just a job. It was personal. His responsibility to Joshua, his desire to protect his son from the darkness that was closing in, had never been more urgent. This case was no longer just about justice—it was about keeping his family safe, even if it meant walking into a storm.

## Forty Seven (47)

As Anna and Cathy continued to explain their findings, Edward's mind kept returning to Joshua. The boy's words echoed in his ears: *I've got you.* But Edward knew that in the world they were stepping into, it wasn't just about having each other's backs. It was about survival.

And as the investigation continued, Edward would do whatever it took to make sure Joshua came out of this unscathed—no matter what the cost.

# Uncovering Naudet's World

The deeper Edward Lucas and his team dug into the disappearance of Jordan Naudet, the clearer it became that this wasn't just a simple missing person case. The world Jordan Naudet had built—his empire, Alliance—was far more than a sustainable energy company. It was a powerhouse of influence, innovation, and most importantly, disruption. Every move Naudet made sent ripples through the global market, and not everyone was pleased with the impact.

---

Jordan Naudet was a visionary, a man whose ambitions extended far beyond the traditional boundaries of business. His company, Alliance, wasn't just a typical corporate entity; it was the embodiment of a transformative approach to global energy consumption and sustainability. Naudet's vision was rooted in the idea that the world could be powered more efficiently, with fewer resources, and that doing so would not only benefit the environment but also generate immense economic opportunities. Under his leadership, Alliance became a major player in the energy sector,

## Forty Seven (47)

challenging conventional wisdom and setting new standards for what was possible.

Founded in Minnetonka, USA, Alliance was created as a forward-thinking energy company with a bold mission: "Generate More, Use Less." The company sought to revolutionize how the world produced and consumed energy, with a particular focus on sustainability and efficiency. While most traditional energy companies were heavily invested in fossil fuels and short-term profit margins, Alliance took a different approach.

Naudet believed that the future of energy lay in renewable resources—solar, wind, and hydroelectric power—and in optimizing energy consumption through cutting-edge technology. Under his leadership, Alliance developed innovative energy grids that redistributed power in more efficient ways, reducing waste and maximizing output. This made the company a key player not only in the U.S. but also on the global stage, as countries around the world began to adopt Alliance's solutions to modern energy challenges.

What made Alliance unique was its focus on long-term sustainability. Naudet wasn't just trying to turn a profit; he was trying to reshape the entire industry. This, naturally, placed him in conflict with more traditional energy companies like ACE, which had built their empires on conventional energy sources such as oil, coal, and natural gas. For Naudet, these outdated models represented the past, and he believed his company would lead the world into the future.

Jordan Naudet wasn't just a businessman—he was a thinker, a philosopher in the world of energy. He had a holistic view of life, always carrying a zippered Bible with him, believing that his work was not only about business but about leaving a lasting, positive impact on the planet. His personal motto, "The life you have always wanted is buried under everything you have," reflected his belief that beneath the layers of consumption and excess, there was a simpler, more sustainable way to live—and he was determined to uncover it.

This belief permeated every aspect of his business strategy. He saw Alliance not merely as a company, but as a movement, one that would eventually push the world towards a greener, more efficient future. His passion was infectious, and it attracted some of the best minds in the industry. Engineers, scientists, and environmentalists flocked to Alliance, drawn by Naudet's vision and the opportunity to work on projects that could genuinely change the world.

But Naudet's visionary leadership style also created challenges. He was known to be uncompromising, demanding the highest standards from his employees and expecting them to share his commitment to the company's mission. Alliance's recruitment process was rigorous, designed to attract only the most qualified candidates. Naudet believed that the key to long-term success was building a strong team—one that could adapt to the constantly evolving challenges of the energy sector.

Alliance's internal structure reflected Naudet's belief in adaptability and innovation. Unlike traditional companies that often became bogged down by bureaucracy, Alliance was lean and nimble. Its employees were encouraged to think creatively and push the boundaries of what was possible. Naudet made it clear that Alliance wasn't a place for those who wanted to play it safe. The company's success depended on its ability to stay ahead of the competition by continuously innovating and improving its processes.

One of the cornerstones of Alliance's approach was the use of cutting-edge algorithms and data analysis to predict market trends and optimize energy production. The company's engineers and data scientists used sophisticated tools like Bezier curves to model energy usage patterns and develop solutions that maximized efficiency while minimizing waste. This allowed Alliance to stay ahead of its competitors, who were often slow to adopt new technologies or resistant to change.

Additionally, Alliance placed a strong emphasis on employee development. Naudet believed that the strength of the company lay in its people, and he invested heavily in job training and development programs. Employees were encouraged to think beyond their immediate roles and to consider how they could contribute to the company's long-term goals. This forward-thinking approach created a culture of constant improvement, where employees were not only focused on meeting current demands but were also looking ahead to future challenges.

One of Alliance's most ambitious projects was its Green Cities initiative, a program designed to help cities around the world transition to more sustainable energy models. The goal was to create urban environments that were powered primarily by renewable energy, with reduced reliance on fossil fuels. The project involved working closely with governments and local authorities to develop infrastructure that could support these new energy systems, from solar panels and wind farms to advanced energy storage solutions.

Through the Green Cities initiative, Alliance made significant strides in changing the way energy was produced and consumed on a large scale. Several cities in Europe, Asia, and North America adopted Alliance's technology, transforming their energy grids and setting new standards for sustainability.

However, Naudet's ambitions extended beyond energy. He also launched numerous social initiatives, such as organizing marathons and charity runs focused on raising awareness about energy conservation and clean water. These events became a symbol of Alliance's commitment to not only transforming the energy sector but also giving back to the community.

But with great ambition came great conflict. As Alliance grew in power and influence, it started to attract enemies. Competitors like ACE, led by the shrewd and calculating Marco Douglas, saw Naudet's company as a direct threat to their business models. While ACE had long dominated the traditional energy market, Alliance's push toward renewable resources was cutting into their profits. ACE's reliance on fossil fuels made them vulnerable to Naudet's innovations, and Douglas was not one to sit back and let his empire crumble.

Douglas had built ACE with a focus on outsourcing and cost-cutting strategies, allowing the company to operate efficiently in the short term. But this approach made ACE less adaptable to the sweeping changes Naudet was bringing to the market. As Alliance grew, ACE struggled to keep up, and tensions between the two companies escalated.

Naudet's rise to prominence wasn't without controversy. His bold initiatives, particularly his efforts to disrupt established markets, made him a polarizing figure. Many traditional energy executives viewed him as an existential threat, someone who was challenging the status quo and pushing too hard, too fast. Lawsuits, public smear campaigns, and corporate espionage were all part of the resistance he faced as Alliance climbed to the top of the energy industry.

Despite the challenges, Naudet remained steadfast in his mission. He was a man of principles, driven by the belief that his work could make the world a better place. But his uncompromising nature also made him enemies, some of whom were powerful enough to stop him.

In the wake of his disappearance, it became clear that Naudet's story was far from simple. His rise to power had been meteoric, but it had also been fraught with tension, conflict, and controversy. As Lucas, Rudra, and Logan investigated the case, they realized that to truly understand what had happened to Jordan Naudet, they would have to delve deep into the world he had built—and the enemies he had made along the way.

***

Edward sat in his office late that evening, staring at the holographic projection on his desk. Alliance wasn't just a company; it was an empire, spanning continents with a network of subsidiaries, partnerships, and exclusive contracts. The company had a singular mission: "Generate More, Use Less." Under Naudet's leadership, Alliance had shifted the focus of energy production toward efficiency and sustainability. They were developing technologies that seemed decades ahead of their competitors, from renewable energy sources to advanced grid systems.

"Alliance isn't just about energy," Lucas said, leaning back in his chair as he spoke to Rudra and Logan on a secure video call. "It's about control. Jordan was using his influence to shape policies and infrastructure, not just in the U.S. but internationally."

Rudra's calm voice came through the speaker. "And that kind of power makes enemies. Energy giants, fossil fuel conglomerates—anyone with a stake in traditional power structures would see him as a threat."

Lucas nodded, agreeing with Rudra's assessment. "Exactly. He wasn't playing by their rules, and that's dangerous. People don't like their profits threatened."

Logan leaned into the screen, looking almost bored. "Let me guess—someone finally got tired of him shaking up the world and decided to take him out?"

Lucas's eyes narrowed. "Maybe. But we need proof. Let's start with the competitors, particularly those who had the most to lose from Naudet's success."

---

One name kept coming up in their investigation: Marco Douglas, the charismatic yet ruthless CEO of ACE, one of Alliance's fiercest rivals. ACE had a very different philosophy when it came to the energy business. While Alliance focused on innovation and sustainability, ACE was built on traditional energy sources and outsourcing practices that maximized short-term profits. Douglas had been vocal in his opposition to the direction Naudet was taking the industry.

Lucas pulled up a profile of Douglas. The man was a corporate juggernaut, having built ACE from the ground up. He wasn't just a businessman; he was a tactician, always looking for the next advantage. His company was deeply entrenched in the energy markets, and Naudet's initiatives were directly threatening ACE's bottom line.

Rudra, who had been digging into ACE's business practices, spoke up. "Douglas is a strategic genius. He's been outsourcing operations internationally, moving manufacturing and services to countries with cheaper labor markets. He's streamlined ACE's supply chains, and he's invested heavily in

## Forty Seven (47)

infrastructure that's designed to undercut Alliance's market share."

"And not just that," Logan added. "He's been known to take an aggressive stance when it comes to competition. Lawsuits, corporate espionage—nothing's off the table for this guy."

Lucas's mind raced as he connected the dots. "So, we've got a man whose company is being threatened by Alliance's advancements. And from the looks of it, Douglas isn't one to back down."

"He's also not one to get his hands dirty directly," Rudra cautioned. "Men like Douglas prefer to operate from behind the scenes."

Lucas leaned forward, his hands clasped together in thought. "Exactly. He won't be the one pulling the trigger, but he could be the one orchestrating it."

***

Marco Douglas was not the type of man to let anyone steal his crown. A shrewd businessman with a reputation for making quick, ruthless decisions, he had built ACE from the ground up. ACE, short for Advanced Competitive Energy, had been the leader in the energy sector for decades, thriving on a traditional model focused on fossil fuels and outsourcing. Douglas had mastered the art of cutting costs, streamlining operations, and staying ahead of regulatory challenges. To him, energy was about power—both literally and metaphorically.

Douglas's rise in the business world wasn't without its struggles. Born into a working-class family, he had clawed his way up through sheer grit and determination. By the time he founded ACE, he had learned the value of outsourcing—using global labor and resources to stay competitive in a market that was always changing. "Outsourcing is the future," he would often say. "It's how you stay lean, stay fast, and stay ahead."

ACE thrived under his leadership, growing into a massive corporation that dominated the energy landscape, especially in the U.S. and Europe. Their business model focused on extracting resources and building infrastructure quickly and cheaply. Douglas was all about profit, efficiency, and growth—no frills, no vision beyond making the next quarter better than the last. In the beginning, that had worked. But then Jordan Naudet and Alliance entered the picture, and everything changed.

Douglas first heard of Naudet through industry whispers. This new player, Alliance, was making waves in renewable energy—something Douglas had always viewed as a niche, not a threat. The notion of "generate more, use less" was, in his eyes, a fad, a trendy buzzword thrown around by idealists. He didn't see the need to pay it much attention, not

## Forty Seven (47)

until Alliance started attracting media attention—and, more importantly, investors.

"Who the hell is this Naudet guy?" Douglas demanded during a board meeting, slamming down a newspaper featuring Alliance's latest renewable energy breakthrough. "Someone tell me why we're hearing so much about this solar, wind nonsense."

Douglas's executives shifted uncomfortably, but one finally spoke up. "He's making waves, Marco. Investors are taking notice. Governments, too. They're talking about subsidizing his projects."

"That's a joke," Douglas scoffed, lighting a cigar. "Renewables don't make real money. They're not scalable, not at the level we are. This Alliance thing will die out."

But as the months passed, it became clear that Alliance wasn't going away. Naudet had managed to create a powerful narrative around sustainable energy—one that resonated not just with governments but with consumers. Douglas's brand of hard, fast business wasn't as appealing to a world growing increasingly concerned about climate change, and Alliance's innovative approach was starting to encroach on ACE's territory.

Douglas wasn't used to losing, and the very idea of being outdone by some visionary upstart ate away at him. His meetings became more tense, his actions more aggressive. He'd always been known for outsourcing, for utilizing cheaper labor from countries like India and China to get the job done faster and cheaper than anyone else. But now, that model was showing cracks. Public perception was starting to shift, with consumers more interested in companies that were making ethical choices, reducing carbon footprints, and investing in sustainable futures.

"Enough with the eco-talk," Douglas snarled at one of his VPs during a heated discussion. "I don't care what Naudet is selling. We're not some hippie organization here. We deal in power—real power."

The VP hesitated. "But Marco, the market is shifting. Alliance is gaining ground. They're even getting ahead of us on some contracts—"

"Then we get them back!" Douglas barked, slamming his fist on the table. "We outbid, outsmart, and outlast them. Make it happen."

Douglas didn't believe in playing fair when it came to competition. Over the years, he had built a reputation for being a cutthroat businessman, known for hostile takeovers and backdoor deals. He had no qualms about using every tool at his disposal to maintain his dominance, and Alliance was no exception.

Alliance's rapid ascent hit ACE in places Douglas never expected—like government contracts. Naudet's Green Cities initiative was particularly problematic. While Douglas was busy optimizing sales and operations with a modernized approach, Naudet was innovating business ideology on a deeper level. His vision of clean energy as the future resonated with cities looking to transition away from fossil fuels. Suddenly, it wasn't just about competition; it was about philosophy, and Naudet's vision was gaining traction.

Douglas was furious. "Naudet's playing to emotions," he spat, pacing in his office. "He's got the media, the governments, and the bleeding hearts eating out of his hand. But we've got the infrastructure. We've got the experience. People want to talk about green energy? Fine. We'll make them see that it's not practical."

But deep down, Douglas knew that Alliance's vision was dangerous. As much as he tried to dismiss it, the writing was on the wall—renewable energy was becoming more viable, and Naudet's innovations in energy grids and sustainability were making it more attractive to investors and consumers alike. Douglas had built ACE on a foundation of power, but Naudet was shifting the ground beneath him.

We should focus on collection of evidences and this must be our research objective. Doubt is often better than over confidence because it leads to inquiry and inquiry leads to investigation. Our Research should also include inductive and scientific thinking and it should promote the development of logical habits of thinking and organizing. It should provide basic for nearly all policies of this investigation our research should also help in solving problems faced related to this crime from time to time and make this case interesting and entertaining. We should also generalize our theories and solve all operational and planning problems of this case. We should seek answers to all problems of this case. Okay territorial god we got it said Rudra. We can also petition the civilians of Minnetonka about Naudet's disappearance said the second brother. Our innovate research should also be territory wise he added. We should innovate this case territorially. We can also make territorial map of online social relationship of Jordan Naudet because his social presence awareness was dreadful. We can also induce technology with camera mediated communication and all other media attributes said Logan. Yeah Jordan's global culture and sub culture has influenced his relationship with online community also Edward replied. We should springer innovation in communication.

We should grab the attention of the information that is relevant, true and verifiable. This is a most important platform to have an attentive audience. By solving this case we increase our detective built up reputation. Our mission should be in our

## Forty Seven (47)

memories. We should remember each and every rigorous swivel of evidences. We should consider the police materials of this law enforcement. We should keep us updated and revised, we should be advanced in our criminological theory.

While this whole discussion was going on Josh was just seeing the newspaper. He came across the word jurisdiction and asked Edward, Dad what is this jurisdiction. Logan said dear question bank, jurisdiction means the official power to make legal judgments and decisions. Jurisdiction can be over cases arising or involving persons residing within a defined region. It can be the region over which an authority one of its courts, or one of its subdivisions has jurisdictions. There are also some jurisdictions that can go something along the lines of beyond regional limits. It can be outside the country's border also. Okay got it Logan uncle said the satisfied kid.

# The Symbol

Josh stood before a large, abstract painting that took up most of the wall in Eduard's flat, the colors and shapes chaotic yet strangely harmonious. His brow furrowed as his eyes traced the lines and curves, unable to decipher the meaning behind the artwork. The image seemed to pulse with energy, as if something ancient and powerful was hidden within it. He couldn't help but feel the weight of its presence in the room.

Logan, who had been standing silently beside him, broke the silence. "What are you looking at, Question Bank?" "Hey don't call me that Logan Uncle" Josh said. "Okay kid, what were you seeing in that painting" said Logan. His voice was light, but there was an underlying curiosity in his tone.

Josh blinked, momentarily pulled from his thoughts. "I don't really get this painting."

Logan smiled slightly, his eyes narrowing in on the artwork with an almost reverent expression. "Boy, that's your father's famous symbol," he said, his voice laced with admiration.

Josh glanced at Logan, confused. "Symbol? What do you mean?"

## Forty Seven (47)

Logan, sensing Josh's confusion, gestured toward the painting. "Do you know by what name your father is known?" he asked.

Josh paused for a moment, the name echoing in his mind. "Oh, you mean 47. But how is this painting related to his name?"

Logan's expression became more serious as he stepped closer to the painting. "Look carefully. The number 47 is hidden in this symbol."

Josh took a step forward, squinting as he examined the painting more closely. The abstract shapes seemed to swirl in a chaotic dance of colors, but as his eyes adjusted, he noticed something peculiar. The design subtly incorporated the number 4 on one side, and a 7 on the other. The more he looked at it, the clearer it became.

Josh's mind raced. "Wait, I see it now. But what's the connection? Why is it here?"

Logan's smile returned, a mixture of pride and knowledge in his eyes. "Your father's symbol isn't just about a number. It's a representation of something much deeper. The 47 isn't just a name—it's a reflection of his mastery over the elements. It's a mark of the power he has harnessed over the very forces that govern our world."

Josh stood still, processing the information. "Elements? What do you mean by that?"

Logan nodded, the weight of his words settling in. "Your father was a master of the five elements—earth, water, fire, air and space. These forces are the building blocks of everything around us, and your father learned to control them, to manipulate them. This symbol represents his connection to them, his understanding of their flow and balance."

Before Josh could respond, Rudra and Eduard entered the room, their footsteps quiet but deliberate. Rudra, always the observant one, raised an eyebrow as he noticed the two men standing in front of the painting.

"What are you two discussing so seriously?" he asked, his voice playful but sharp.

Josh glanced at Logan before turning back to Rudra. "We were talking about the symbol. About the number 47 and how it's connected to the elements."

Rudra's eyes flickered with recognition. "Ah, yes. The 47. I see Logan has already started teaching you about it." He smiled, though there was a depth to his expression that suggested he was about to share something significant.

Josh nodded, eager to learn more. "I'm trying to understand it. But there's still a lot I don't get."

Logan gave him a knowing look. "Don't worry, Josh. It's not easy to grasp at first. But once you understand the basics, everything else will start to make sense."

Rudra stepped forward, placing a hand on Josh's shoulder. "Let me break it down for you," he said, his voice steady and calm. "The first element is earth."

Josh raised an eyebrow, clearly intrigued. "Earth? But that's just... well, the planet we live on, right?"

Rudra chuckled softly. "Yes, in a way, but it's much more than just the ground beneath our feet. Earth is the foundation, the physical body. It's the substance that holds everything together. Without it, we wouldn't exist. It's not just the soil or the rocks, but the very bones of your body, the flesh you inhabit. It's the substance that gives you form."

Josh took a deep breath, processing Rudra's words. "So, earth is like... our mother?"

Rudra nodded. "In many ancient traditions, earth is considered the mother of all. In Bharatiya culture, for example, the earth is revered as our mother, the source from which we emerge and to which we eventually return. The biological mother is just a representation of this larger force, this universal force."

Logan added, "That's right. When we eat, we consume the earth. The plants we harvest, the food we eat—they all come from the earth. And how we treat the earth, how we treat the land, directly reflects how we treat ourselves. The earth is the source of all life, and we are connected to it more deeply than most people realize."

Josh nodded slowly. "That makes sense. But what about the other elements?"

Rudra smiled. "Next comes water. It's an element that most people underestimate, but it's perhaps the most important."

Logan picked up the conversation. "Water is everywhere. It makes up most of our bodies, and it flows through us just as it flows through the rivers and oceans. Without water, there's no life. But water isn't just about survival. It's about balance. Water represents emotion, fluidity, adaptability. It's both calming and destructive, depending on how we treat it."

Josh raised his hand. "So, when we drink water, we're not just nourishing our bodies, we're also connecting to this element?"

Logan nodded. "Exactly. And not just that. The way we interact with water, the way we allow it to flow through us, affects our emotions and our energy. If you hold onto your emotions, if you stop the flow of water within you, it stagnates. And just like stagnant water, your energy becomes toxic."

## Forty Seven (47)

Rudra added, "In ancient practices, water was also seen as a memory keeper. It doesn't just carry nutrients—it carries information. Your thoughts, your intentions, your very soul are reflected in the water around you. It holds the memory of everything, every experience."

Josh, his eyes wide with wonder, said, "Wow, that's powerful. So water is like... a mirror?"

"Yes," Rudra replied. "Water reflects not only what's around it but also what's within you. If you can learn to master it, you can master your own emotional world."

Logan continued, "After water comes air—the element of movement and thought. Air is the breath of life. It's what fuels your body and mind. When you breathe in deeply, you're taking in not just oxygen, but the very essence of life. It clears your mind and strengthens your spirit."

Josh inhaled deeply, feeling the air fill his lungs. "So air is about freedom and clarity?"

"Exactly," Rudra said. "With air, you can clear away the fog, both mentally and spiritually. Air is the force that connects us all. It's the energy that powers our thoughts, our words, and our actions."

Josh felt a surge of excitement. "I'm starting to understand. But what about fire?"

Logan's eyes lit up at the mention of fire. "Ah, fire. The most fascinating element of all."

Rudra smiled at Josh's eager expression. "Fire is the element of transformation. It's the force that burns away the old, clearing space for the new. Fire represents passion, energy, and the drive to create. It's the spark that ignites change and the heat that forges strength."

Josh's mind raced with possibilities. "So, fire is about transformation and change?"

"Exactly," Rudra said. "Mastery over fire isn't just about creating destruction—it's about harnessing that energy and using it to fuel your journey. The fire within you is the source of your ambition, your purpose, your drive to move forward."

Josh felt the weight of Rudra's words settle within him. For the first time, he understood the elements not just as abstract concepts but as forces that governed everything in his life. The 47 symbol wasn't just a name—it was a blueprint for mastery over the universe itself.

And now Joshy it's whole day since morning you are troubling us. You should now have dinner and get to sleep. Because if we continue to answer you we will get bankrupt serving your Question Bank, so please now leave us. Okay my three mystery men said Josh.

## Forty Seven (47)

As he stood there, taking in everything Logan and Rudra had shared with him, Josh felt a deep sense of purpose stirring inside him. He wasn't just the son of 47. He had the potential to become something more—to master the elements and unlock the power that lay dormant within him.

Next morning Josh woke up before time and sat with his mother Brenna. He told her that last day he had an interesting journey with his Dad and uncles about the mystics of five elements of body and universe. And today they will tell me more about these. So Joshy what did you understood from last day discussion asked Edward when he joined Brenna along with his two friends.

Josh said the boundaries of body are very limited. But boundaries of the mind are larger. As our knowledge expands our mental boundaries can expand. Yeah and we ended the discussion on elemental fire said Rudra. He continued by saying if you become conscious of dimension of elemental fire, you will be a boundless being, because the elements play across the entire creation.

We can do physical work, mental work and if we do something with our body, it has a certain lifespan. Things we do with our mind have a slightly longer lifespan. If we do something with our life giving source it has a much longer life but once you work beyond this physical dimension that is forever. No one can destroy it. We three friends have never any spirituality, but we are crystal clear about anything concerned with human consciousness. Everything that we know, we do not know. But when I want it, it is always there. This is how people are using the internet today you do not have to carry the information with you. It is all there. We can access it whenever we want all beings who have broken all dimensions of barriers within themselves and touched the ultimate-what they perceived, grasped and distilled within themselves is for always. This internet can be called as inner net. You just have to access it.

There is an individual mind and there is a universal mind. They are just a reflection of each other. It is just that the individual mind may be too muddled and it may not be catching all of it. If one is able to access life though the akashic (Space) mind i.e. the fifth element instead of the individual you see not only possible situations for yourself, you see possible situations for just about anything. But the problem is that if you even as much as talk about these things all kind of people will start imagining all the different types of nonsense.

Akasha i.e the space is also carved in the symbol of 47. You see the circle covering the numbers 4 and 7 symbolizes the space element which contains every aspect that exists in this universe.

## Forty Seven (47)

There is a simple process to Tap into the Akashic Mind. Today modern science is recognizing that there is something called as akashic intelligence, that is, empty space has a certain intelligence. Whether this intelligence works for you or against you will determine the nature of your life. Whether you are a blessed being or, One who is going to be knocked around for the rest of your life. Some people seem to be hammered around by life for no reason while others seem to be blessed with everything. It is not for no reason. It is our ability - either consciously or unconsciously - to be able to get the cooperation of this larger intelligence which is functioning.

In this context, one important aspect of spiritual progress and science is to perceive beyond five senses that which we call sixth sense, which is physical in nature and explore the mystical nature of our existence i.e. enhancing the akasha. These six senses are also indicated on the symbol of 47. The six dots on the circle made by the numbers 4 and 7 are combinedly called six senses. The circle indicates the fifth element i.e. the akasha.

Our five senses - sight, sound, smell, taste and touch are also based on five elements of nature which are governed by the functioning of organs - eyes, ears, smell, taste and touch.

Ears or hearing is the quality of the ether element.

Skin or touching is related to the earth element.

Tongue or taste is the quality of the water element.

Nose or smell is related to the air element.

Eyes are the vehicle for the fire element.

Lastly it our sixth sense which also helps us get those good and bad feeling before planning anything or taking a big step forward. There are many things sixth sense can do.

And you see that seven in the symbol. This seven belongs to your "father's love" your mom. Your father believes that "Love is the seventh sense that guides you to the sixth sense" and love towards anything a user cannot find in its user manual. He has this feeling of love or strong attraction towards your mother. Indeed he loves what he does every single minute of his life.

"Thanks," Josh said, his voice thick with newfound understanding. "I think I'm starting to get it."

Logan smiled warmly. "Good. Now the real journey begins."

# The National Rally for Jordan Naudet

The city of Minnetonka had never seen a gathering quite like this. What started as a quiet plea for justice had evolved into an overwhelming demonstration of community unity. The rally to support Jordan Naudet was a testament to the strength and resilience of the people who believed, as fiercely as Edward Lucas did, that the truth would not remain hidden forever. It was a cry for justice that echoed through the streets, drawing people from all walks of life, bound by a singular purpose — to bring Jordan Naudet home and ensure that those responsible for his disappearance were held accountable.

As the sun began to set, painting the sky with shades of orange and gold, the first wave of attendees trickled into the designated meeting point. The crowd grew steadily, a blend of familiar faces and strangers, all united by the cause. Some arrived in the casual comfort of jeans and T-shirts, their bodies adorned with slogans demanding justice for Jordan. Others wore more formal attire, perhaps sensing the weight of the occasion, as if the very fabric of their clothes had to reflect the gravity of the rally they were attending.

Tattered banners and hand-painted signs fluttered in the cool evening breeze, their vibrant colors bright against the dusky backdrop of the city streets. Each sign carried a different message, but all were anchored in the same sentiment — *We want justice. We want answers.*

Edward Lucas, the famed detective at the heart of the investigation into Jordan's disappearance, stood silently at the front of the crowd. His gaze swept over the sea of faces, taking in the faces of the young and old, the quiet and the outspoken, the citizens of Minnetonka and the surrounding areas. He was aware of the immense weight of expectation resting on his shoulders. These people were not just rallying for a cause; they were rallying for the life of someone they loved, someone whose fate had been thrust into the uncertain hands of fate, and it was his duty to find the answers they sought.

"We won't rest until we find him!" The shout came from the back of the crowd, raw and defiant, echoing off the walls of the nearby buildings. The words were met with loud applause and a chorus of affirmations. The voice that had cried out was a stranger to him, but their passion felt familiar. The same urgency he saw in their eyes was mirrored in his own heart. This was not just a rally for Jordan; it

## Forty Seven (47)

was a collective statement that Minnetonka would not allow itself to be complacent in the face of injustice.

The march began, winding its way through the heart of the city. The people, once strangers to one another, were now bound by their shared purpose. Edward walked at the head of the crowd, flanked by his allies, Rudra and Logan. Their steps matched the rhythm of the gathering, and Edward found himself momentarily lost in the sea of humanity. There was something stirring in the air, a feeling of unity that had not existed before. For the first time since Jordan's disappearance, he felt like he wasn't alone in his quest for justice. The crowd, with its chants and its energy, had become a powerful ally.

"We need to gather as much evidence as possible," Edward spoke aloud, the urgency in his voice reflecting the need to keep moving forward. His eyes scanned the crowd as they marched, looking for any small detail, any face, any clue that might help. "Every piece of information, no matter how small, could be crucial."

Rudra, ever vigilant, nodded in agreement, his eyes darting from one person to the next, alert to any shift in the crowd, any sign that might point them in the right direction. "Agreed. But we need to stay focused. We're close to something, I can feel it."

Logan, always the more reflective of the trio, added his own thoughts. "It's about more than just the facts. It's about understanding the bigger picture. What do we know about Jordan? Why did he vanish? What's the motive behind all this?"

Edward paused, considering Logan's words. "I don't think this is a random act. Whoever took Jordan has a purpose. The question is, what is that purpose? And why hasn't anyone come forward with any information?"

As the march continued, Edward found himself caught in a deeper contemplation about the nature of crime itself. It wasn't just a matter of solving the puzzle. It was about understanding why the puzzle existed in the first place. "Crime is a symptom," he muttered, almost to himself. "It's the consequence of something deeper—inequality, corruption, a failure in our society to address the real issues."

Rudra's voice cut through his thoughts. "And if we're going to stop this from happening again, we need to understand those roots. We need to go beyond the surface level."

The rally was growing in strength, its momentum matching the rising sense of purpose among those who had gathered. The people weren't just marching for Jordan Naudet anymore. They were marching for the soul of their community, for the integrity of their lives, for justice. And for Edward

## Forty Seven (47)

Lucas, the need to unravel the mystery had never felt more urgent.

As they reached the center of the city, the rally's crescendo could not be ignored. Edward stepped forward, taking his place at the makeshift stage set up for the speeches. His voice, steady and resolute, rose above the crowd.

"We stand here today not as individuals," Edward began, his voice carrying the weight of their collective hope, "but as a united community. We are here to demand justice. We will not rest until every stone has been turned, every lead followed, and every truth uncovered."

The crowd responded immediately, an overwhelming roar of approval that rattled the ground beneath them. Their chants filled the air as the people of Minnetonka raised their voices in unison. "Bring him home! Bring him home!" The sound reverberated through the city, carrying with it the promise of persistence and a refusal to be ignored.

Edward allowed himself a moment of pride, but only a moment. The work was far from done. The investigation was still ongoing, and the truth, however close it seemed, remained just out of reach. Yet, for the first time since Jordan's disappearance, Edward felt that they might just be closer to the answer. Not because of any new evidence or breakthroughs, but because of the collective will of the people behind him.

Behind him, Rudra and Logan exchanged glances, their silent acknowledgment of the battle ahead clear in their eyes. Together, they were a team. And no matter the challenge, they would face it head-on.

"We are in this together," Edward continued, his voice rising again, "and together, we will find Jordan Naudet. Together, we will bring him home."

The crowd erupted once more, and for the briefest of moments, the air around them felt lighter. It wasn't just the relief of collective action; it was the weight of their commitment to truth, to justice, to one another.

As the rally began to wind down, the crowd slowly dispersed, leaving behind a sense of purpose that would linger long after the event had concluded. But for Edward Lucas, the real work had only just begun. The march had been a reminder of the power of the people, but it had also been a call to action. Jordan's case was far from closed, and there was still so much to uncover.

Edward knew that the road ahead would be long and fraught with danger, but with the support of Rudra, Logan, and the rallying cry of the people echoing in his ears, he felt more determined than ever. The fight for justice was not over. It was just beginning.

## Forty Seven (47)

With renewed strength and unwavering resolve, Edward Lucas prepared for the next phase of the investigation. The truth was waiting. And no matter what, they would find it.

To boost morale, 47 reminded his team that the biological system, the brain, and the Earth itself operate on the same frequencies, implying that Naudet couldn't have simply vanished—he would be found. Rudra, one of his mates, was surprised by this insight, prompting Logan, the more intelligent of the two, to explain that it was a quote from Nikola Tesla. Rudra responded with a strong, "Oh."

# The Media's Role: Anna Thomas and Areus News

The bustling newsroom of Areus News hummed with activity as journalists rushed to meet deadlines and prepare for the day's broadcasts. Among them was Anna Thomas, a seasoned correspondent known for her fearless reporting and unwavering dedication to uncovering the truth. Anna Thomas, a seasoned correspondent for Areus News, was no stranger to covering high-profile cases and breaking news stories. With a career spanning over a decade in investigative journalism, Anna had earned a reputation for her tenacity, resourcefulness, and unwavering commitment to uncovering the truth.

Born and raised in a bustling metropolis, Anna's passion for storytelling was ignited at a young age. Growing up in a family of journalists, she was exposed to the power of media in shaping public discourse and holding those in positions of authority accountable. Inspired by the stories of courage and resilience she encountered through her parents' work, Anna knew from an early age that she wanted to pursue a career in journalism.

## Forty Seven (47)

After graduating from college with a degree in journalism, Anna embarked on her professional journey, eager to make her mark in the world of news reporting. She started her career as a cub reporter at a local newspaper, where she honed her skills in investigative journalism and cultivated a keen eye for detail.

Over the years, Anna's career trajectory took her to various news outlets, where she covered a wide range of topics, from local politics to international conflicts. Her fearless approach to reporting and relentless pursuit of the truth earned her accolades from her peers and solidified her reputation as a respected journalist in the industry.

It was Anna's reputation for excellence that caught the attention of Areus News, a prestigious media conglomerate known for its in-depth coverage of global events. Hired as a correspondent for the network, Anna quickly distinguished herself with her ability to deliver compelling stories that resonated with audiences worldwide.

When news broke of Jordan Naudet's mysterious disappearance, Anna's journalistic instincts kicked into high gear. Sensing the significance of the case, she immersed herself in the investigation, determined to uncover the truth behind Naudet's vanishing.

Drawing on her extensive network of sources and contacts, Anna tirelessly pursued leads and conducted interviews, leaving no stone unturned in her quest for answers. Her relentless pursuit of the truth garnered attention from both the public and law enforcement agencies alike, positioning her as a key figure in the ongoing investigation.

As the case gained momentum, Anna's reporting became instrumental in keeping the public informed and engaged. Her investigative pieces provided crucial insights into the intricacies of the case, shedding light on the various theories and developments that emerged over time.

Anna sat at her desk, poring over notes and scanning through news articles, her mind abuzz with the latest developments in the case of Jordan Naudet's disappearance. As one of Areus News's top reporters, she knew that she had a crucial role to play in bringing the story to light and holding those responsible to account.

"Anna, we need you in the studio in five minutes for the morning briefing," called out her producer, snapping her out of her reverie.

With a quick nod, Anna gathered her notes and made her way to the studio, her heart pounding with anticipation. As she took her seat in front of the camera, she focused her thoughts and prepared

## Forty Seven (47)

to deliver the news to millions of viewers across the country.

As Anna Thomas addressed the camera, her words carried the weight of urgency and purpose. "Good morning, everyone. I'm Anna Thomas, reporting on the latest developments in the case of Jordan Naudet's disappearance," she began, her voice steady and unwavering.

"Since Jordan Naudet was reported missing ten days ago, there has been a significant lack of progress in the investigation. However, new leads have emerged, shedding light on potential avenues for further inquiry," Anna continued, her eyes scanning the teleprompter for the latest updates.

"As authorities continue their search for answers, questions loom over the circumstances surrounding Naudet's last known whereabouts. Reports suggest that he was last seen in a park in Minnetonka, but the details surrounding his disappearance remain shrouded in mystery," she explained, her tone tinged with a sense of urgency.

"As we await further updates from law enforcement, it is crucial that we, as a community, remain vigilant and continue to keep Naudet and his family in our thoughts. With each passing day, the need for answers grows more pressing, and it is incumbent upon all of us to do our part in the search for truth," Anna concluded, her gaze unwavering as she addressed the camera with a sense of determination.

She launched into a detailed report, outlining the latest findings and speculating on possible leads in the investigation. With each word, she knew that she was playing a vital role in keeping the public informed and putting pressure on authorities to take action.

As the broadcast drew to a close, Anna's phone buzzed with a message from her editor, urging her to dig deeper into the story and uncover any new leads. With a sense of determination, she set to work, reaching out to her network of sources and scouring through every available piece of information.

Days turned into weeks, and still, Anna remained relentless in her pursuit of the truth. She conducted interviews with witnesses, sifted through mountains of evidence, and pieced together a timeline of events leading up to Naudet's disappearance.

But just as she felt like she was getting closer to cracking the case, she hit a roadblock. Key sources began to clam up, and crucial pieces of evidence seemed to disappear into thin air. Frustration gnawed at her, but Anna refused to give up.

Then, one day, a breakthrough came in the form of a tip from an anonymous source. They claimed to have information that could blow the case wide

## Forty Seven (47)

open—a revelation that sent shockwaves through the newsroom and sent Anna scrambling to verify its authenticity.

With her adrenaline pumping and her heart racing, Anna followed up on the tip, conducting interviews and cross-referencing details with other sources. Slowly but surely, a clearer picture began to emerge, and Anna knew that she was onto something big.

As she prepared to go live with her latest report, Anna felt a sense of pride and satisfaction wash over her. She had worked tirelessly to uncover the truth, and now, she was finally ready to share it with the world.

"Good evening, everyone, and welcome back to Areus News," Anna began, her voice ringing out with authority. "Tonight, we have a major breakthrough in the case of Jordan Naudet's disappearance."

She launched into her report, revealing the shocking details of her findings that there are a evidences of a suspicious taxi and a taxi driver in the park in which Naudet was last seen and laying out the evidence for all to see. As she spoke, she knew that she was making a difference—that her reporting was shining a light on the darkest corners of society and holding those responsible to account.

And as the broadcast drew to a close, Anna couldn't help but feel a sense of satisfaction knowing that she had played a part in bringing justice to Jordan Naudet and closure to his loved ones. For Anna Thomas, the pursuit of truth was not just a job—it was a calling, and one that she would continue to follow with unwavering dedication and determination.

Forty Seven (47)

# The People's Movement

The disappearance of Jordan Naudet sent shockwaves through the entire nation. It was more than just a missing CEO—Naudet had become a beacon of hope for those advocating for a sustainable future. His work at Alliance Energy had inspired people across the globe, from government officials to ordinary citizens, who saw in him a visionary committed to solving the planet's most pressing issues. As the founder of the company, he wasn't just leading a business; he was leading a revolution in green energy, pushing for a future where environmental sustainability took precedence over corporate greed.

When his family announced his disappearance, it became more than a headline—it was a national crisis. News outlets scrambled to cover every angle, and within hours, his face was everywhere: television screens, smartphones, and newspapers. The bold red headline of "MISSING" followed his sharp features on every front page. Jordan Naudet, the man who had once championed the idea of a green future, had vanished. The world, especially those who had placed their trust in his vision, was left grappling with what his disappearance meant for the future of the planet.

Headlines read like a forewarning:

- "Where is Jordan Naudet? The Missing Energy Visionary"
- "Alliance Founder Mysteriously Vanishes—Foul Play Suspected"
- "The Architect of Green Energy Disappears: A Conspiracy Unfolding?"

By seeing these headlines in newspapers and television 47 whispered to his friends "I would kill to see this Naudet guy."

The news dominated the airwaves, but it wasn't just about the mystery of a missing man—it was about the future he represented. For those who followed his work, Naudet had come to symbolize a better tomorrow, one where sustainable energy could thrive alongside economic growth. His absence felt like a seismic shift in the ideals many had rallied around.

As the story unfolded, the public's concern grew. The authorities seemed slow in their investigation, and people became restless. Vigils sprang up across the country, the largest one outside the glass towers of Alliance's headquarters in Minnetonka. Hundreds gathered, candles in hand, faces illuminated in the soft glow of flickering flames.

# Forty Seven (47)

The atmosphere was filled with unease, frustration, and deep sorrow.

"I don't understand how someone like him could just vanish," Clara McKinney, a former Alliance PR employee, said, her voice quivering. Her eyes, though tired, reflected the weight of the uncertainty. "Jordan was always there, always pushing for something better. And now... he's gone?"

Naudet was more than just a CEO. To many, he was a modern-day hero, a man whose ideals had transcended traditional business practices. His company, Alliance, wasn't just about profit—it was about reshaping the world's energy systems for the betterment of future generations. His disappearance threatened to undo all the progress he had worked so tirelessly to build.

The growing unrest was palpable. Angry murmurs began to rise among the crowd.

"Why aren't the authorities doing more?" a voice from the back shouted.

"They're dragging their feet," another person called out, their frustration seeping into the words.

The public's anxiety soon became something more than mourning—it was an outcry for justice. People demanded answers. The media machine turned into an insatiable beast, hungrily pursuing every lead, every possible theory.

Anna Thomas, an investigative journalist known for her fearless pursuit of truth, took center stage. With her signature blend of determination and passion, Anna quickly became the voice of the people, the one who refused to let the case fade from the spotlight. Standing outside Alliance's headquarters during a live broadcast, she spoke with conviction: "I'm not convinced this is just another missing person case. There's more to this story, and we owe it to the public to find out what happened to Jordan Naudet. His work meant something to a lot of people."

Her words resonated with viewers who were hungry for answers. Unlike many of her colleagues, Anna didn't stand behind a desk. She was out in the field, talking to the people, uncovering layers of the mystery. Her investigative instincts led her to the heart of the story, interviewing former colleagues, friends, and even enemies of Naudet.

In one emotional segment, Anna sat down with Ethan Cooper, a former project manager at Alliance. His eyes were hollow, a reflection of the weight he carried over his missing friend.

"Jordan wasn't just a boss," Ethan said, his voice breaking. "He cared about what he was doing. He wasn't in it for the money. He genuinely believed he could change the world. And now... he's just gone?"

Anna leaned forward, her expression gentle yet inquisitive. "Did he ever express concern? Did he feel threatened by anyone?"

Ethan shifted, his unease evident. "There were always rumors... you can't be as successful as Jordan without making some enemies. Especially with Marco Douglas and ACE breathing down his neck."

That name—Marco Douglas—immediately grabbed attention. Douglas, the CEO of ACE Energy, had long been a rival of Naudet's, and his name stirred the growing narrative of corporate espionage. Had Douglas, or someone connected to him, been involved in Naudet's disappearance?

The public's attention was now fully focused on the case. Protests began to swell, initially in small groups but quickly growing into a nationwide movement. In major cities across the country, thousands of people took to the streets, holding signs and chanting for justice.

In New York, the streets were filled with protesters bearing signs like:

- "Find Naudet, Save Our Future"
- "Justice for Jordan"
- "No Green Without Naudet"

The energy in the air was electric, palpable, with each rally only growing in size and intensity. The movement was no longer just about a missing person—it had evolved into a demand for transparency and accountability. People wanted the truth, no matter the cost.

At one of the largest rallies in Washington D.C., speakers from environmental groups took the stage, honoring Naudet's contributions to sustainability and climate change efforts. Corporate leaders shared their admiration for Naudet's ability to blend innovation with ethical practices. The sense of loss was profound, but the will for justice was stronger.

One young activist, barely twenty, stepped up to the microphone, her voice shaking but unwavering. "Jordan Naudet wasn't just a CEO. He was hope for a better future. We need to know what happened to him. We can't let his disappearance be brushed under the rug."

This speech sent waves through the crowd, strengthening the resolve of those already protesting and inspiring even more to join the cause. The energy, the urgency, was undeniable.

The pressure on law enforcement mounted. It was no longer enough to issue vague statements. The people demanded action. The FBI, the police, and the government were under immense scrutiny.

# Forty Seven (47)

Despite their reassurances, the public was not satisfied.

At one tense press conference, an angry protester shouted from the back of the room, "You've had weeks! Where's Naudet?"

The law enforcement officials stood firm, but their composure was cracking under the weight of public expectation. Each passing day without new leads only deepened the sense of urgency.

In the midst of this storm, the Naudet family who hired Edward Lucas, known as 47, a private investigator with a reputation for solving the unsolvable was also worried. His team, along with Anna Thomas, dug into the case with precision, their search for answers becoming even more critical as time ticked on.

With every passing day, the story continued to grow. What began as the mysterious disappearance of a businessman had now become a national cause. The people were speaking, the movement was swelling, and the pressure on those in power was undeniable. Jordan Naudet's future, the future he had envisioned, hung in the balance. His vision was too important to be swept away in silence. And the people weren't going to let that happen.

# The Burning Man and The Unraveling

Josh, who had been playing, came to talk to his parents. "I want to go to the Burning Man festival because my friends are going."

Brenna asked, "What is Burning Man?"

Eduard explained, "Burning Man is a week-long desert event focused on community, art, self-expression, and self-reliance. The name comes from its culminating ceremony—the symbolic burning of a large wooden figure, which could be a person, an animal, or a symbolic figure known as an effigy. The event takes place at Black Rock City and follows ten principles: radical inclusion, gifting, decommodification (which emphasizes social entitlement), radical self-reliance, radical self-expression, communal effort, civic responsibility, leaving no trace (LNT—promoting conservation and proper waste disposal), participation, and immediacy. At Burning Man, participants design and build all the art and events, including experimental sculptures, interactive installations, and art cars. It's an extraordinary event that encourages creative expression in many forms."

## Forty Seven (47)

Brenna said, "That sounds interesting. We should attend this event tomorrow."

The next day, Eduard, Brenna, and Josh went to Black Rock City for the Burning Man event. Eduard purchased three tickets upon arrival. The venue was filled with numerous theme camps and art installations. The event was well-organized, bringing together artists and audiences in a unique way. The Burning Man figure stood 85 feet tall.

Additionally, there was the Temple, a significant recurring installation at Burning Man, considered just as important as the Man. The Temple was a neutral, non-denominational spiritual space for personal reflection and community gatherings. It was not a religious temple but a place for remembering the past, honoring the present, and envisioning the future. People could leave words and objects behind to be burned, creating a space for contemplation, rituals, weddings, and reunions. The Temple, called the "Temple of Direction," was inspired by Japanese shrines and would be burned on the eighth and final night of the festival, following the burning of the Man.

The festival's theme was "Dream," and the Temple featured an intersection of culture, technology, and nature. Josh participated in climbing activities, and he witnessed a humorous moment when another child became afraid at a certain height and started crying, while his mother cheered him on.

As night fell, the festival came alive with fire and LED artwork. Creative expressions included music, performances, and theater. Hundreds of artworks, ranging from small to large-scale, were displayed, with the Artery department of the Burning Man Project assisting in placing and lighting them to ensure safety.

The highlight of the evening was the Burning Man itself—an art car shaped like an octopus, dramatically modified and set on fire. This art car represented the burning away of old memories and the emergence of new possibilities. As the festival drew to a close, the crowd began to disperse, and the event concluded with the doors of Black Rock City closing, marking the end of an extraordinary day.

Eduard commented that the event was a smashing success. "All that careful preparation and creative artistry during the event were definitely worth watching," he said.

"Did you like the event, Josh?" Brenna asked.

"Yeah, I loved it," Josh replied. "It was very entertaining and amusing."

"Let's head back to Minnetonka," Eduard suggested. The group boarded their transport and returned to

## Forty Seven (47)

Minnetonka that night to resume their daily routines.

The following day, after arriving at the flat, the two friends inquired about Eduard's family's thoughts on the event. Josh enthusiastically shared, "It was amazing. I saw the Burning Man and a burning octopus car too."

"Wow, that sounds interesting," Logan remarked. "In our country, we also burn a dummy demon every year."

"Really?" Josh asked. "What's the demon called?"

"The demon is called Ravana," Logan explained. "We burn it with modern fireworks as well."

"Wow, would you take me to Bharat to see it?" Josh requested.

"Yeah, sure, why not?" Rudra, the elder brother, agreed.

After settling down from the event, the three friends convened for an important meeting about Naudet's disappearance. It was a critical moment in the ongoing investigation.

"Police officials have shared some significant news with the help of surveillance cameras," Logan began. "Surveillance cameras play a vital role in crime fighting," Eduard added.

"We've found surveillance footage that may be related to Naudet's suspected murderer," Eduard continued. "The footage shows a taxi driver placing four trash bags into his taxi around the park. If Naudet was in one of those bags, what about the other three?"

The two brothers speculated, "The other bags might just be trash to avoid suspicion."

"Very clever," Eduard said. "But this surveillance footage could help us solve the crime. Criminals don't seem to outsmart technology for long, and as technology advances, so does our ability to catch them. The world is becoming safer each day, thanks to CCTV cameras that routinely help solve crimes. Surveillance cameras can catch criminals in the act and leave them scrambling."

Eduard continued, "We need to analyze fragments of the footage from different cameras and angles to identify the culprit and solve Naudet's disappearance. Surveillance videos are crucial for identifying suspects and their eventual capture. We know Naudet went to the park that evening, and multiple cameras show him wandering there. We should also look for the protruding finger among the trash bags. It's crucial that we have everything ready in three or four days."

The air in the car was thick with adrenaline and tension as 47, Logan, and Rudra drove through the winding road toward their target. Edward Lucas, better known as 47, had pieced together clues leading them to the location of the man he believed could blow the case of Jordan Naudet's disappearance wide open. This was their moment to strike, but as with most things in their line of work, nothing ever went according to plan.

The team pulled up to an abandoned warehouse on the outskirts of the city, its shadow looming ominously against the pale moonlight. The faint hum of machinery from inside suggested they were not alone. 47 stepped out of the car, his sharp eyes scanning the perimeter. He signaled for Logan and Rudra to follow, their weapons at the ready.

Inside, the air smelled of rust and oil. The dim lighting cast eerie shadows across the walls. They moved silently through the labyrinthine structure, each step calculated, their breaths shallow.

Suddenly, a glint of metal caught 47's eye—a gun, poised and aimed directly at Logan's back. The man holding it stood hidden behind Logan, his movements calculated and precise.

"Logan," 47 hissed, his voice steady but urgent, "bend down!"

Logan glanced over his shoulder, a confused smirk on his face. "This is hardly the place for seeking blessings from you, boss," he quipped, his voice laced with his usual sarcasm.

Before 47 could retort, a shot rang out.

The man with the gun stumbled backward, clutching his chest as blood spread across his shirt. Behind him stood Rudra, his pistol still smoking. "No one messes with my team," Rudra muttered, his voice low and dangerous.

"Rudra!" 47 roared, striding toward the fallen man. "What have you done? He was our only link to Jordan Naudet and Marco Douglas!"

Logan chimed in, ever the source of unwelcome commentary. "Well, now we've killed to see him."

"Shut up, Logan," Rudra snapped, his eyes narrowing.

47 crouched beside the lifeless body, running a hand through his hair in frustration. The lead was gone. Their chance to find Jordan Naudet and uncover the truth about Marco Douglas had slipped through their fingers. He clenched his fists, the weight of their failure settling heavily on his shoulders.

---

Back at his office, 47 sat at his desk, his head bowed. The usually unflappable detective looked defeated. The quiet hum of the city outside felt like a cruel

## Forty Seven (47)

contrast to the chaos swirling in his mind. Losing the lead was a devastating blow, and with every passing second, he felt the case slipping further from his grasp.

His team worked around him, trying to piece together the remaining fragments of the investigation, but the mood was grim. That was until the door burst open, and a young hacker named Zara stormed in, a victorious grin plastered across her face. In her hand, she held a small but potent weapon: a USB drive.

"47," she announced, practically breathless, "we've got a new lead."

The room fell silent as everyone turned to her. Zara was one of the best hackers in the business, and her tenacity had paid off. She placed the USB drive on 47's desk with a sense of triumph.

"I managed to hack into Marco Douglas's network," Zara explained, her voice a mix of excitement and urgency. "It wasn't easy—his security is top-notch—but I found something. Emails, encrypted messages, financial records, all tied to Alliance and Jordan Naudet. It's all here."

47's eyes lit up with a glimmer of hope. He picked up the USB drive and held it as if it were the key to unlocking the mystery. "What's in there?" he asked, his voice steady but eager.

Zara pulled up a laptop and plugged in the drive. The screen flickered to life, revealing a labyrinth of files. Her fingers danced across the keyboard as she decrypted the data.

"This," she said, pointing to the first document, "is a series of deleted emails between Douglas and several unnamed associates. They discuss sabotage plans—delays in Alliance projects, bribes to officials, and even threats to Naudet himself."

The room was silent as Zara continued. "Here's another thread," she added, opening a series of encrypted messages. "It's between Douglas and someone using the alias 'Shadow.' They're talking about an 'opportunity to remove Naudet from the picture permanently.'"

47 leaned in, his sharp eyes scanning the screen. "Do we know who this 'Shadow' is?" he asked.

"Not yet," Zara admitted, "but I'm working on it. What's more important is this—financial records." She opened another file, revealing transactions worth millions of dollars. "Douglas has been funneling money into offshore accounts and paying off high-level officials to cover his tracks. But these payments? They correspond to dates right before Naudet's disappearance."

Rudra stepped forward, his brows furrowed. "So, we're looking at a conspiracy? Douglas wasn't just a rival—he orchestrated this?"

## Forty Seven (47)

"Exactly," Zara confirmed. "And there's more. I found files on a property Douglas owns outside the city. It's remote, heavily secured, and completely off the grid. If Naudet is alive, that's where they're holding him."

47 straightened, a renewed sense of purpose washing over him. "We need to move fast. If Douglas knows we're onto him, he'll cover his tracks."

Logan, who had been uncharacteristically quiet, finally spoke. "What's the plan, boss? Do we go in guns blazing, or do we play this smart?"

47 smirked. "Smart. We can't afford to make another mistake. Zara, I need you to keep digging. Find out everything you can about this property—security systems, access points, anything."

"You got it," Zara said, already typing furiously.

"Rudra, Logan," 47 continued, turning to his team, "we're going to need a tactical approach. Gather the gear and map out our strategy. We're not just rescuing Naudet; we're taking down Douglas and his entire operation."

The team sprang into action, their earlier disappointment replaced by determination. Hours stretched into days as they prepared for what would undoubtedly be their most dangerous mission yet.

The breakthrough had injected new energy into the investigation. Zara worked tirelessly, uncovering more details about Douglas's operation. Each piece of evidence painted a clearer picture of a man willing to do anything to maintain his power, even if it meant eliminating his greatest rival.

As 47 stood by the window of his office, watching the city lights flicker in the distance, he felt a sense of resolve. The case was far from over, but for the first time in weeks, he felt like they were finally gaining the upper hand.

"Douglas won't see this coming," he muttered to himself, a steely determination in his voice.

With the USB drive in his possession and his team by his side, 47 knew one thing for certain: justice for Jordan Naudet was within reach. And this time, he wouldn't stop until the truth was laid bare for the world to see.

# Inferno and Pursuit

The air in the temporary office reeked of burnt coffee and stale exhaustion. Edward Lucas, or simply 47 to his team, sat surrounded by shattered faces and frayed nerves. Zara had managed to hack into Marco Douglas's corrupt network and retrieve a treasure trove of incriminating data, which now sat on a small but invaluable pen drive in Edward's jacket pocket. The team should have been celebrating, but an unshakable sense of dread hung over them.

"Double-check the encryption," Edward instructed Zara as he paced the room. "If Douglas realizes what we've got before we're ready, he'll throw everything he has at us."

He didn't know how right he was.

A quiet knock on the door pulled everyone's attention. Before anyone could respond, the door swung open, and a man stepped in—a stranger, seemingly ordinary in appearance but with an unsettling calm in his demeanor. He smiled, unzipping his jacket to reveal an explosive vest strapped to his chest.

"Good evening," the man said, his voice chillingly pleasant. "You've been making quite a mess of things. My employer sends his regards. You've got 40 seconds to decide—save your people or your precious evidence."

For a moment, the room stood frozen. Then Edward's voice rang out, sharp and commanding.

"Everyone, move! Get out now!"

His team didn't need to be told twice. They scrambled toward the exit as the bomber chuckled, glancing at the countdown on his vest. **39... 38... 37...** Zara hesitated, her hands hovering over her laptop.

"The data!" she exclaimed. "We'll lose it all!"

"I'll handle it," Edward growled, grabbing the pen drive and shoving it into his jacket. He pushed Zara toward the door. "Go!"

The timer ticked down as Edward swept his gaze over the office, ensuring everyone had evacuated. He sprinted toward the stairwell just as the timer hit zero. The explosion ripped through the building, a deafening roar that shattered glass and sent a wave of heat tearing through the floor. Edward barely made it outside, his body slammed to the ground by the force of the blast.

# Forty Seven (47)

From the vantage point of a nearby rooftop, Edward and his team stood transfixed, their faces illuminated by the fiery inferno that had once been their office. The flames roared with a ferocity that felt almost sentient, consuming everything they had built—equipment, files, and months of relentless work. Smoke billowed into the night sky, blotting out the faint glimmers of stars.

The air was thick with acrid fumes, but none of them moved. None of them spoke. The sound of approaching sirens grew louder, but it was drowned out by the thunderous roar of the fire.

Edward's hand instinctively reached into his jacket. His fingers brushed against the smooth surface of the pen drive, still nestled securely in the inner pocket. Relief flooded him for a brief moment, only to be replaced by a cold, simmering fury.

"Someone leaked our location," he muttered, his voice almost drowned by the chaos but cutting through the tension like a blade. His words weren't a question; they were a statement of fact, and the venom in his tone left no doubt about his anger.

Logan, coughing into his sleeve to ward off the smoke, helped Zara to her feet. Her face was streaked with soot, her hair a mess, but her eyes were filled with equal parts terror and guilt.

"That's an understatement," Logan said grimly. He glanced at the burning building, his jaw tight with frustration. "This wasn't random. They knew exactly where to hit us."

Edward straightened, his shoulders squared despite the weight of exhaustion and loss pressing down on him. The flickering light of the fire reflected in his eyes, turning them into molten steel.

"We're not done," he said, his voice low but resolute. "Douglas thinks he can scare us off? He has no idea what's coming."

---

Across the city, in a dimly lit penthouse perched high above the skyline, Marco Douglas paced like a caged predator. The office smelled of leather and expensive scotch, but the tension was suffocating. He held the phone so tightly that his knuckles turned white.

"You're telling me he survived?" Douglas's voice was a growl, his usual calculated demeanor shattered by disbelief and fury. His free hand slammed onto the glass desk with a resounding crack, sending a crystal tumbler tumbling onto the floor.

The voice on the other end of the line hesitated. "Y-yes, sir. Lucas escaped the explosion. And..."

"And?" Douglas barked.

"And... he managed to save the pen drive."

## Forty Seven (47)

For a moment, there was silence. A dangerous, suffocating silence that stretched for too long. Then Douglas exhaled sharply, his nostrils flaring as he fought to regain control of his spiraling rage.

"The pen drive," he repeated, his voice cold now, devoid of the earlier fury. "The one with everything on it?"

"Yes, sir," the voice confirmed, trembling.

Douglas leaned back in his chair, the leather creaking under his weight. He rubbed his temples, his mind racing. He had underestimated Lucas. That much was clear. But this wasn't over—not by a long shot.

Slowly, a smile crept across his face. It was not a smile of humor or relief; it was the predatory grin of a man who had just concocted a cruel, brilliant idea.

"Send the Man Eater," he said, his voice almost a whisper but carrying the weight of an execution order.

"Sir?"

Douglas leaned forward, his eyes gleaming with malicious intent.

"Lucas wants a fight," he said. "Let's give him one he won't survive."

As he hung up the phone, the room fell silent again, save for the faint crackle of ice in his abandoned scotch glass. Somewhere in the shadows, a figure stirred—a hulking, monstrous silhouette that seemed almost too large to be human.

The Man Eater was ready.

---

The Man Eater was more myth than man. Stories of his brutality circulated in hushed whispers even among hardened criminals. He wasn't merely an enforcer—he was destruction incarnate. His towering frame, clad in black combat gear, seemed almost too large to fit through the shattered doorway of the safe house. A chill rippled through Edward's team as they caught sight of him. His eyes gleamed like a predator's, locked immediately on Edward.

"Get back!" Logan yelled, raising his pistol with trembling hands.

The Man Eater didn't flinch. He moved with terrifying speed for his size, closing the distance in an instant. Logan barely got a shot off before the brute's arm swung like a wrecking ball, sending him crashing into a table that splintered under the impact.

## Forty Seven (47)

"Logan!" Zara screamed, but Edward grabbed her arm.

"Move!" he barked, shoving her toward the rear exit.

The Man Eater's gaze never left Edward, his steps deliberate as he stalked forward. His voice, deep and guttural, rumbled like distant thunder. "You have something that belongs to Mr. Douglas."

Edward didn't wait to respond. He hurled a chair at the advancing figure, buying himself precious seconds as he bolted for the back door. The Man Eater batted the chair aside like a toy and gave chase, his boots pounding against the floor with a force that rattled the walls.

---

The alley was narrow, lit only by flickering streetlights. Edward leaped onto his parked motorcycle, his hands fumbling with the ignition as adrenaline surged through his veins. The engine roared to life just as the Man Eater exploded out of the doorway behind him, shards of wood scattering like shrapnel.

Edward twisted the throttle and shot forward, the tires screeching against the pavement. He glanced over his shoulder, his stomach sinking as he saw the Man Eater mount a dirt bike with practiced ease.

"You've got to be kidding me," Edward muttered under his breath.

The chase tore through the city, a whirlwind of chaos and destruction. Edward weaved through narrow streets, his motorcycle leaning precariously as he rounded sharp corners. Cars honked and swerved as the two blurred past, the Man Eater closing the gap with every passing second.

Edward's mind raced as fast as his bike. *Think. He's faster and stronger. Outmaneuver him.*

Spotting an abandoned construction site up ahead, Edward veered sharply, skidding through the entrance and into the labyrinth of steel beams and scaffolding. He ducked under low-hanging pipes, the confined space forcing him to slow down.

The Man Eater followed without hesitation. Unlike Edward, he didn't bother to dodge obstacles. Metal scaffolding buckled and collapsed as he plowed through, his dirt bike roaring like an unrelenting beast.

Edward cursed under his breath. "Does this guy ever stop?"

Realizing he couldn't outrun him forever, Edward brought his bike to a screeching halt in an open section of the site. Dismounting, he turned to face his pursuer, his fists clenched at his sides.

## Forty Seven (47)

The Man Eater approached with a smirk, his massive boots crunching over gravel. He abandoned the dirt bike and cracked his knuckles, the sound echoing ominously in the still night air.

"You've made a mistake, Lucas," he growled.

Edward didn't respond. He launched himself forward, throwing a series of quick jabs aimed at the Man Eater's midsection. His fists landed with dull thuds, but the brute barely flinched. Instead, he swatted Edward aside with a backhanded blow that sent him sprawling to the ground.

Edward rolled to his feet just in time to dodge a crushing stomp that left a crater in the dirt. He pivoted, using his smaller frame to his advantage, darting around the Man Eater and aiming for weak points—knees, elbows, and the side of the head.

The Man Eater grunted as a particularly well-placed kick forced him to stagger, but his recovery was swift. He grabbed a length of rebar from the ground and swung it like a baseball bat. Edward ducked, the whoosh of the metal slicing through the air inches from his head.

The fight was brutal, a clash of skill versus raw power. Edward's movements were calculated, but the Man Eater's strength was overwhelming. Every missed strike from the brute tore chunks of concrete from the ground, sending debris flying.

Finally, the Man Eater feinted, drawing Edward into close range. With a roar, he wrapped a massive arm around Edward's torso, lifting him off the ground and slamming him into a steel pillar. The impact knocked the wind out of him, and Edward crumpled to the ground, gasping for breath.

The Man Eater reached into Edward's jacket, his hand closing around the pen drive. Edward's eyes widened as the brute held it up, a smug grin spreading across his face.

"You think you've won?" Edward rasped, struggling to stand.

The Man Eater didn't reply. Instead, he opened his mouth and swallowed the pen drive whole, his throat bulging as it went down.

Edward stared in disbelief. "You've got to be kidding me."

---

### The Finale

Before the Man Eater could savor his victory, the sound of approaching sirens filled the air. Blue and red lights danced against the walls of the construction site as the SWAT team arrived, their weapons trained on the towering figure.

## Forty Seven (47)

The Man Eater turned, his expression darkening. "You called backup?"

Edward smirked, wiping blood from the corner of his mouth. "No, but they're always fashionably late."

The SWAT team moved in with precision, deploying nets and non-lethal rounds to subdue the brute. The Man Eater roared, tearing through the first net with sheer strength. He charged at the officers, but a second net ensnared him, followed by a tranquilizer dart that finally brought him to his knees.

Edward watched as the monster fell, his breathing ragged but victorious.

As the SWAT team secured the Man Eater, one of the officers approached Edward. "We'll need to extract that drive from him. It might take some time."

Edward nodded, his gaze fixed on the unconscious brute. "Take all the time you need. Just make sure it's intact."

For now, the fight was over, but Edward knew the war against Douglas was far from won.

# The Weight of Knowledge

The small flat felt unusually suffocating. 47 sat hunched over on the edge of the couch, his head bowed low, his hands clasped tightly. Across from him, Logan and Rudra sat silently, their faces mirroring the weight of the moment. Edward leaned against the wall, staring out the window, his thoughts as distant as the skyline he watched. The room, though filled with people, felt empty—a stark reflection of the hope that had drained from their mission.

The loss of evidence was a blow none of them had anticipated. All their efforts, every lead painstakingly followed, had led them to a moment of triumph—and just as quickly, it had slipped through their fingers. The fiery chaos of the day still lingered in their minds, a haze of smoke, destruction, and missed opportunities.

"All gone," 47 muttered. His voice broke the silence, but it carried no weight, no conviction. It was as if he couldn't believe his own words.

"We'll figure something out," Rudra offered, but even he sounded unsure. His usual optimism felt hollow in the face of their defeat.

## Forty Seven (47)

Logan exhaled heavily, running a hand through his hair. "We've been through worse," he said, though the words seemed directed more at himself than anyone else.

47 didn't respond. His mind replayed the events of the last few days like a broken record, each repetition deepening the sense of failure.

The stillness of their shared misery was broken by the sudden sound of the door creaking open. Josh, Edward Lucas' adopted son, bounded in, his school bag slung over one shoulder and a textbook clutched in his hands. His carefree energy was a sharp contrast to the somber mood that filled the room.

"Uncle Logan!" Josh called out, oblivious to the tension. "Look at this—"

Before he could finish, his foot caught on the edge of the rug. He stumbled, and the book slipped from his hands, landing with a soft thud on the floor.

"Careful, kid!" Logan snapped, his tone sharper than he intended.

Josh froze, his eyes wide as he looked between Logan and the fallen book. "I didn't mean to—"

Logan sighed, his initial irritation fading as he leaned forward to pick up the book. He dusted it off carefully, his hands lingering on its cover. "It's not about meaning to, Josh. It's about respect."

Josh tilted his head, puzzled. "Respect? For a book?"

Logan leaned back, the book still cradled in his hands as if it were something precious. "Books aren't just things, kid. They're knowledge. And knowledge... well, it's the most powerful thing you'll ever have."

"But it's just my math book," Josh said, frowning slightly.

Logan chuckled softly. "It doesn't matter what kind of book it is. Math, history, fiction—they all teach us something. In our culture, books have always been sacred. You know why?"

Josh shook his head, his curiosity piqued.

"In ancient Bharat," Logan began, his voice taking on a reverent tone, "books were more than tools for learning. They were treasures. People carried them on their heads, like crowns, to show respect. Knowledge wasn't just something you learned—it was a gift from Saraswati, the goddess of wisdom. And gifts from the gods deserve to be honored."

Josh's eyes widened. "So that's why we say sorry when we step on a book?"

Logan nodded. "Exactly. When you accidentally touch a book with your foot, it's like being careless with something sacred. Apologizing shows you understand its value. It's not just a custom—it's a way of being thankful that knowledge has chosen to be with you."

Josh considered this, his gaze falling to the book in Logan's hands. Slowly, he reached out and took it, holding it carefully. Then, in a gesture both earnest and endearing, he placed the book gently on his head. "Like this?"

Logan smiled, pride glinting in his eyes. "That's the spirit."

"Smart kid," Rudra added with a grin.

Josh beamed at the praise, then scampered off to his room, the book now clutched to his chest like a prized possession.

---

The room felt heavy with an unspoken weight, an oppressive silence lingering in the air. 47 sat hunched on the couch, his elbows resting on his knees, eyes focused on nothing in particular. The dull hum of the refrigerator and the distant sounds of the city outside were the only noise breaking the stillness. But the quiet wasn't comforting—it was a reminder of everything they'd lost, every ounce of progress they had made that had evaporated in the blink of an eye. The evidence was gone, the plan derailed. He could almost hear the echoes of failure creeping into the corners of the room, squeezing the air out of his lungs.

Logan, who had been pacing the room, stopped and leaned back against the wall, exhaling a long, tired breath. He rubbed his face, as though trying to shake off the weariness. His eyes, usually sharp and perceptive, were clouded with frustration, but there was also something else in them. A quiet, stubborn determination. He couldn't let this moment define them.

"Sometimes, you can learn a lot from kids," Logan said, breaking the silence with the suddenness of a thought he'd been holding on to. His voice was low, almost a murmur, but it carried through the room with surprising clarity.

47 didn't look up immediately. His gaze remained fixed on the floor, his hands clenched tightly in his lap. The words didn't register at first—his mind still too tangled in the mess they had found themselves in. But after a beat, he looked up, meeting Logan's eyes for the first time in what felt like hours. His face was still heavy with frustration, his eyes shadowed with self-doubt. "Like what?" he asked, his voice thick, as though every word was weighed down by the burden of the day.

Logan's eyes softened, and he pushed himself off the wall, walking over to the couch. "Like how to bounce back." He nodded towards the door where Josh had just disappeared after his little misstep with the book. "Josh didn't cry over dropping his

## Forty Seven (47)

book. He picked it up, learned from the moment, and moved on. Maybe we need to do the same."

47 stared at him for a long moment, the words sinking in slowly, as though Logan had just thrown him a lifeline he hadn't realized he needed. But still, doubt lingered in his chest, and the despair hadn't fully left him. "You really think that's enough? Moving on from this?" he asked, his voice a low growl, tinged with the frustration that had been gnawing at him for so long.

Logan met his gaze head-on. "What else are we going to do, 47? Sit here, wallowing in our failure while Douglas gets away with everything? While our whole world crumbles because of one mistake? That's not who we are. That's not what we stand for."

Rudra, who had been silently watching the exchange, finally spoke up, his voice calm and grounded. "Logan's right. We've been through worse. Yeah, we lost the pen drive, but we still have our brains, our team, and our determination. Douglas hasn't won yet. Not by a long shot."

It was the simplicity of the words that hit 47 hardest. He had been so focused on the immediate loss, the tangible thing they couldn't get back, that he had forgotten to look at the bigger picture. They still had the things that mattered most—the skills, the resolve, the will to fight. They had each other. That was more than enough.

"And we've got each other," Logan added with a small, wry grin, his hand running through his hair in that habitual gesture of his. "And Josh's math book, apparently."

A faint smile tugged at the corners of 47's lips. It was small, almost imperceptible, but it was there. And that alone felt like a small victory. He hadn't realized how badly he needed that reminder—how easily he had gotten lost in the weight of everything. His eyes flickered towards the hallway, where he could still hear the soft patter of Josh's footsteps retreating.

Logan leaned in, his voice dropping to something more serious. "Look, we've been fighting for this long, right? For the truth. For justice. For people who don't even know we're out here. We're not about to let one setback end everything. We still have everything we need to keep going. You just have to believe that."

47's gaze turned inward, the weight of his thoughts pressing down harder than ever before. For a moment, he let himself be consumed by the darkness—the feeling of being so close, only to have it all slip away. But then he realized something. Logan was right. They still had their minds, their strength, and each other. That was their

## Forty Seven (47)

foundation. And nothing—no setback, no failure—could take that away.

He sat up straighter, his shoulders squaring, and for the first time in hours, he felt something shift inside of him. It wasn't a complete change, not yet. But it was the start of something. The resolve he had been searching for began to take root. It wasn't the end. It couldn't be.

"You're right," he said, his voice quieter now, but firm. "We still have what matters most. And as long as we have that, we have a chance."

Logan gave him a long look, as if measuring the sincerity in his words. Then, a slight nod, the kind that said more than words ever could. "Exactly."

Rudra, too, gave him a reassuring smile. "We'll figure this out. Together."

The air in the room shifted again. It wasn't as heavy as before. There was still a long road ahead, and no one here was fooling themselves into thinking it would be easy. But for the first time in days, 47 felt something flicker inside of him—hope, maybe, or at least the will to keep pushing forward. And that was enough.

As the silence stretched out, it wasn't oppressive anymore. It was contemplative, thoughtful. They weren't just sitting in defeat anymore. They were planning. They were strategizing. And more importantly, they were starting to believe that they could do this.

47 exhaled, a deep breath that felt like he was shedding a weight he hadn't even realized he'd been carrying. "Alright," he said, pushing off the couch, his movements more purposeful now. "Let's get to work."

Logan grinned, a familiar spark in his eyes. "Now that's the 47 we know."

Rudra chuckled softly, shaking his head. "Let's just hope this plan involves more than just a math book."

There was a brief flash of laughter, light and genuine, something that had been missing for far too long. And in that moment, 47 knew that this wasn't the end. Not even close.

---

The knock at the door came just as they were beginning to piece together their thoughts. Zara peeked her head in, her expression hesitant but determined.

"I didn't mean to interrupt," she said, stepping inside, "but I think I found something."

All eyes turned to her, the weight of their shared defeat momentarily forgotten.

"What is it?" Rudra asked, leaning forward.

## Forty Seven (47)

Zara held up a tablet. "While you were dealing with the Man Eater, I kept digging. There's a trail—a faint one, but it's there. It might lead us to a backup of the data we lost."

47 stood, his posture firm and commanding. "Show me."

As Zara began to explain her findings, the room filled with a renewed sense of purpose. The fight wasn't over—not by a long shot. This time, they wouldn't just protect knowledge; they would wield it like the powerful weapon it was, ensuring that no obstacle could keep them from uncovering the truth.

For the first time in days, hope flickered in their hearts. And 47 knew, deep down, that this was just the beginning of their resurgence.

# A Moment of Solitude

The night was deep, an ocean of quiet broken only by the soft ticking of the clock on the wall. 47 stood in the center of his small apartment, a place he had once found solace in, but now it felt suffocating—distant, cold. The faint lights from the street below filtered through the blinds, casting long shadows that seemed to stretch into the very depths of his mind. He had lost everything. Or at least that's how it felt. He could almost feel the crushing weight of failure pressing against his chest.

Logan, Rudra, and Edward had all gone to bed hours ago. There had been no fight over it; everyone knew that, after a day like today, they needed rest. Even the most resolute needed to sleep. But sleep had become a stranger to 47. How could he rest when the truth was slipping further from his grasp with each passing second? How could he sleep when he felt like the very thing he had dedicated his life to—justice, truth, and uncovering the dark corners of the world—was slipping through his fingers like sand?

He didn't know what he was doing anymore. It wasn't just the case, the evidence, the elusive figure of Marco Douglas. It was everything. His purpose,

## Forty Seven (47)

his path—it all seemed hazy and indistinct now, a blur of wasted effort, lost leads, and broken promises. The burden of it all pressed so heavily on him that he could barely breathe.

He glanced over to the small table beside the couch. There, nestled in the corner, was the Bible. A reminder of a simpler time, a time when things made sense. When life had meaning, and faith—whether in a higher power or in the good of people—was enough to carry him through. But faith had begun to feel distant. He hadn't touched the Bible in years, had barely even thought about it. But tonight, standing in the wake of his failure, he reached for it, his fingers brushing against the worn leather cover. It felt foreign, like a relic from a past life, but it was still there—still waiting for him.

47 slowly sank into the couch, the Bible resting open in his hands, as if it had called him there. His gaze wandered over the pages, the words that had once comforted him now a jumble of distant memories. He couldn't remember the last time he had prayed. The last time he had truly believed that there was something beyond this world to guide him.

"God..." He whispered the words softly, his voice barely audible in the room. "I don't even know what I'm asking for. I don't know if I still believe in you, or if I even believe in anything anymore. But I need help. I need direction. This case is tearing me apart. And I don't know how to keep going. What am I supposed to do when everything seems to fall apart around me? Where do I go when the path forward is so unclear?"

The silence of the room felt like it was swallowing him whole. He closed his eyes, fingers still gripping the edges of the Bible. The weight of the world was on his shoulders, and he had no idea how to lift it. He had been so close to solving the case, so close to putting an end to Marco Douglas's reign of terror. But now, after everything had been lost, he found himself grasping at straws, desperate for any sign of hope, any kind of answer.

He let out a long, shaky breath, his body sagging with the exhaustion that had plagued him for days. He didn't expect an immediate answer, not from a book, not from anything. But in that moment, he just needed something. Something to keep him moving, to keep him from falling into the abyss.

"Please," he murmured again, his voice trembling. "Just... show me something. Anything. Give me a sign. A reason to keep going."

For a long while, there was nothing. No dramatic change, no voice in his head, no sudden illumination. Just the same darkness. Just the same crushing weight. It felt like his plea had been swallowed whole, lost to the wind. But even so, he

## Forty Seven (47)

didn't close the Bible. He didn't give up. He let the pages fall open to a random verse, not caring what it was, just hoping for some small piece of solace, some tiny glimmer of light.

His fingers landed on a passage from the Book of Psalms. *"The Lord is my shepherd; I shall not want. He maketh me to lie down in green pastures: he leadeth me beside the still waters. He restoreth my soul..."*

The words seemed to float on the edge of his mind, filling the room with a strange kind of peace. He had heard them a thousand times before, but tonight, they felt different. Tonight, they felt like a lifeline—a thread he could follow, even in the darkness.

His thoughts drifted as he continued reading, a sense of calm beginning to seep into him despite the storm raging in his mind. *"Yea, though I walk through the valley of the shadow of death, I will fear no evil: for thou art with me; thy rod and thy staff they comfort me..."*

It was the first time in days that he felt a flicker of hope, even if it was faint. A reminder that there was something greater than the immediate chaos, something that could provide comfort when everything else seemed lost. Maybe he didn't have all the answers, and maybe the path forward wasn't clear, but there was still something out there—still something worth fighting for. Maybe that was enough.

47 closed his eyes, the Bible resting gently in his hands. He wasn't sure what had changed in him, but something had. Maybe it was the words themselves, or maybe it was just the simple act of asking for help—of reaching out, even when he didn't believe. For the first time in days, he felt a small seed of resolve take root in his chest. Maybe it wasn't all over. Maybe there was still a way forward.

He opened his eyes and glanced around the room. It felt different now. Less oppressive. The silence wasn't as heavy, and the shadows seemed to retreat into the corners, no longer stretching to consume him. The weight of the world wasn't gone, but it felt a little lighter. A little more bearable.

47 stood slowly, the Bible still in his hands, and for the first time in what felt like forever, he felt like he had a purpose again. He didn't know how everything would unfold, and he didn't know how he would bring Marco Douglas to justice, but for the first time in a long time, he felt like he had something to fight for.

He knew he wasn't alone in this battle. And for the first time, that was enough.

He set the Bible down on the table, glancing at the door. The night had grown quiet again, but this

## Forty Seven (47)

time, it felt like a space where he could breathe. 47 walked toward the kitchen, his movements slower but purposeful, his mind already beginning to form a plan. There was work to be done, and he wasn't going to let the darkness consume him again. Not tonight.

As he reached for a glass of water, he heard the soft shuffle of footsteps behind him. He turned to see Logan, standing in the doorway, his face etched with concern.

"You okay?" Logan asked, his voice low and cautious.

47 gave him a small smile, one that didn't quite reach his eyes but carried with it a sense of quiet resolve. "Yeah," he said softly. "I'm okay. I think I've finally figured it out."

Logan raised an eyebrow but didn't press him. He simply nodded. "Good. We've got work to do."

47 nodded back, his mind already sharp, the faintest glimmer of hope now a steady flame. The case wasn't over. Not yet. And as long as there was breath in his body, he wasn't about to give up.

The night might have been dark, but there was light at the end of the tunnel, and he was going to find it.

# Dream into Reality

The night stretched endlessly, and in the dim light of his apartment, 47 sat back on the couch, the Bible still in his hands. His mind swirled with thoughts of failure, of lost leads, and of a case that seemed increasingly impossible to solve. Despite everything, he couldn't shake the feeling that there was still something more to be discovered, something just out of reach. He closed his eyes, his body heavy with fatigue, but his mind raced as though it couldn't rest. His fingers slowly traced the edges of the Bible, an object that had never failed to give him solace in times of doubt.

Tonight, however, it was more than just a source of comfort. It felt almost like a lifeline—one that he had grasped in desperation after losing so much. The pages felt warm against his hands, as though they had absorbed every prayer, every plea for guidance that had ever been whispered into them. Without thinking, he slid down, adjusting his position on the couch. He didn't want to sleep, not because he feared rest but because sleep had never been kind to him. It brought too many dreams—too many visions of things he couldn't understand, things he couldn't control. But tonight, the

## Forty Seven (47)

exhaustion weighed too heavily, and with a quiet surrender, he laid the Bible under his head like a pillow while thinking of his son.

His last thought before sleep enveloped him was a silent prayer: *Please, show me the way. Please, help me see what I'm missing.*

The moment his head touched the Bible, a sense of peace washed over him. The weight of the world lifted slightly, and his body surrendered to sleep, even as his mind still lingered on the case, on Marco Douglas, on the shadowy figures lurking in the dark corners of the investigation. The night, however, was not to be kind.

As sleep claimed him, the world around him began to shift. The apartment faded, the quiet hum of the city was replaced by the eerie stillness of a vast, open space. At first, 47 thought it was just another dream, another fleeting vision. But something about this one felt different. It felt real. More than real. It felt like something he was meant to see, something that was being shown to him for a reason.

He stood in the middle of a barren, desolate land. The ground was cracked, dry, and lifeless, stretching as far as his eyes could see. The air was thick, heavy with the weight of forgotten secrets. In the distance, there was a mansion, tall and imposing, casting long shadows over the land. The mansion was a dark, looming structure—its windows darkened and its doors shut tight, as though it had been abandoned for years. But 47 knew better. This was Marco Douglas's mansion. The heart of it all. The source of the chaos, of the corruption, of everything that had brought him to this point. And yet, it was so much more than that. This place, this mansion, it held the answers he sought. It was where the truth was buried. It was where he would find the missing piece of the puzzle.

And then, as if summoned by his thoughts, a figure appeared before him, standing in the middle of the barren land. It was a spade. Not a man, not a person, just the tool—a spade, buried halfway into the ground, as if someone had started digging but abandoned the task halfway through. The sight of it sent a chill down his spine. The spade seemed to hum with energy, as though it were connected to something far greater than itself. Something ancient. Something powerful.

The moment 47 laid eyes on it, he felt a sudden surge of understanding. The spade. The land. The mansion. It was all connected. A key. A symbol. A clue to the next step in his investigation. The spade was no ordinary tool; it was a sign. A symbol of something buried, something that had been hidden beneath the surface for far too long.

## Forty Seven (47)

47 reached out for it, his hand trembling as his fingers wrapped around the cool metal. The moment he touched it, the ground beneath him trembled, and the vision around him seemed to shift. The mansion grew larger, more imposing, and the land seemed to stretch out even further, as if pulling him deeper into its grasp. The spade in his hands felt heavier now, its weight almost unbearable, as though it had absorbed the entire burden of the secrets it had been entrusted with.

He tried to pull it free from the earth, but the spade resisted. It was as if the ground itself was holding it back, refusing to let go of what it had buried. The mansion loomed behind him, its dark windows watching him, its silent gaze piercing through him like an unseen eye. There was something watching. Something waiting.

Suddenly, the vision shifted again, and he was no longer standing alone in the barren land. Now, there were figures moving around him—shadows in the distance, their faces obscured, their movements quick and jerky, like they were being pulled by some invisible force. The air grew colder, the tension rising in his chest as he felt a growing sense of urgency.

He needed to act. He needed to dig. The spade was the key, and the mansion was the destination. He knew it, without a doubt. Everything he had been searching for—the truth, the answers—was hidden beneath the earth, beneath the land that Marco Douglas had claimed as his own. The mansion, the land, the spade—it was all connected, and he had to uncover what lay buried.

He dropped to his knees, digging with all his strength, his hands gripping the spade as he plunged it into the ground. With each thrust, the earth seemed to resist him, but he kept going. His hands were raw, his muscles aching, but he couldn't stop. He had to keep digging. He had to find what was hidden.

As he dug deeper, the vision around him began to warp and twist. The shadows grew darker, more threatening, and the mansion behind him seemed to shift, its windows now glowing with an eerie, unnatural light. The figures in the distance were getting closer now, their forms taking shape. He could hear their footsteps, the soft shuffle of movement in the distance. They were coming for him.

And then, just as he thought he might be overwhelmed by the forces around him, the earth gave way. The spade struck something solid. Something heavy. He couldn't see it yet, but he could feel it—a presence, an energy, a weight. The spade had uncovered something buried deep within the earth.

## Forty Seven (47)

He pulled it free, his hands shaking as the object was revealed. It was a box. A small, metallic box, its surface scratched and dented from years of neglect. It was old—so old—but it pulsed with energy, as if it had been waiting for this moment, waiting for him to uncover it.

47's heart raced as he reached out to open the box. The lid creaked as it moved, revealing a stack of papers, old photographs, and a series of documents, all marked with the same symbol: the logo of Marco Douglas's company. It was all there—the evidence, the truth, the thing that had been buried for so long.

As his fingers traced over the documents, a voice echoed in his mind—soft, almost like a whisper. *"You've found it. The truth. But it's not over. You've only just begun. The real work starts now."*

The vision shifted again, and 47 was suddenly standing in front of Marco Douglas's mansion. The door creaked open, and a figure stood in the threshold—Marco himself, tall and imposing, his eyes cold and calculating.

"You think you've won?" Marco's voice was low, mocking. "You've only just scratched the surface."

And with that, the vision shattered, and 47 was jerked back into reality. He woke up with a start, his body drenched in sweat, his heart pounding in his chest. For a moment, he was disoriented, confused, unsure of where he was. But then, as the fog of the dream cleared, he realized what had just happened.

The vision had been real. The spade, the mansion, the box—it was all part of the investigation. It wasn't just a dream. It was a sign. A vision of what he needed to do next.

He sat up slowly, his mind racing. He had the key now. He knew what he had to do. The spade had uncovered something—something that had been buried for far too long. And Marco Douglas wasn't going to let him walk away from this.

But 47 wasn't afraid anymore. He had a purpose. He had the truth. And now, he was going to bring it to light, no matter the cost.

# The Unveiling American Dream

The dawn was just beginning to break when 47's eyes snapped open, his heart racing, a cold sweat still clinging to his skin. The vision, that dream, whatever it had been—it was so vivid, so real. The spade, the mansion, the box—it all made sense now. It was as though the pieces of the puzzle had clicked into place, and the weight that had been hanging over him for days, weeks even, suddenly felt a little less burdensome.

He took a deep breath, trying to steady himself. The truth was right there, just within his grasp. It was as if the universe had reached out to him in the form of a dream, guiding him to the next step. He couldn't afford to waste any more time. Marco Douglas, the man who had orchestrated so much of the corruption, the violence, the darkness—it was time to finally bring everything to light.

With his thoughts racing, 47 quickly rose from his couch, the Bible still tucked under his arm. He couldn't help but smile faintly. *The Bible,* he thought. *A strange but fitting guide.*

His mind was already on the task at hand. He grabbed his phone, dialed Logan and Rudra's numbers, and within moments, both of them answered.

"We need to move," 47 said, urgency in his voice. "I know where Naudet is."

The phone line crackled with disbelief.

"What?" Rudra's voice was thick with sleep but tinged with immediate curiosity. "How? What do you mean, you know where Naudct is?"

"I'll tell you everything, just get ready," 47 replied. "We're going to Marco Douglas's mansion. I know where the evidence is. I know where the truth is buried."

He hung up quickly, not giving them a chance to respond. He was already gathering the essentials—his jacket, his bag, and his most trusted tool: a metal detector. The device was going to be crucial. He knew exactly what to look for now, and the metal detector would help them pinpoint it, no matter how deeply it had been hidden beneath the earth.

By the time Logan and Rudra arrived to face Edward, 47 was ready. His eyes burned with determination, his mind sharp and focused. There was no room for hesitation now.

## Forty Seven (47)

"What the hell is going on, 47?" Logan asked, his tone half-amused, half-confused as he walked through the door. He quickly took in the serious air about 47 and the equipment laid out before him. "You know where Naudet is? How?"

"I'll explain on the way," 47 replied. "Let's get to the mansion first. Time is critical."

Rudra and Logan exchanged looks, but neither of them questioned 47's resolve. They knew when he was certain about something, and right now, he was sure of one thing—he had found the next clue. He had found the path forward.

The three of them piled into Logan's car, and the journey to Marco Douglas's mansion began. The sky was still tinged with the colors of early morning—light pinks and oranges that seemed to promise a new beginning. But for 47, there was no time for promises. He was chasing something far more urgent: the truth.

Rudra's voice broke the silence, cutting through 47's thoughts.

"Okay, please. You've been holding back. What's really going on here?"

47 didn't answer immediately. His fingers tightened around the steering wheel, his knuckles white. He knew the question was coming, but it didn't make answering it any easier. How could he explain

something so... surreal? The dream had been so vivid, so real, but how could he convince his friends that the answer to solving Jordan Naudet's murder and bringing down Marco Douglas was hidden in the dirt of his estate?

He glanced at Rudra in the rearview mirror, then at Logan, who sat beside him in the passenger seat. Both of them had been silent since they left 47's apartment. Rudra's brow was furrowed in confusion, while Logan's expression was unreadable—he had that quiet skepticism about him that had always been there whenever they found themselves chasing something wild, something inexplicable.

As they drove, 47 finally explained.

"I dreamed of a mansion," 47 began, his voice low but steady. "It was Marco's mansion. I saw a spade, buried in the ground, and somehow, I knew that the spade was the key. It's how Marco buried Jordan Naudet. I think... I think the truth is buried out there. And we need to find it."

There was a brief moment of silence. Rudra stared at 47, as if trying to make sense of the words he had just spoken. Logan, on the other hand, just let out a low chuckle, shaking his head.

"Seriously?" Logan's voice was laced with disbelief. "This is the plan now? We're following a dream?"

## Forty Seven (47)

47's gaze hardened, his eyes still locked on the road ahead. He could feel Logan's skepticism, but he couldn't afford to let it derail him. Not now. Not when they were this close.

"I know this sounds crazy," 47 admitted, his tone firm but resigned, "but trust me, this is our next and only hope. I can't explain how, but everything in my gut tells me that this is it."

Rudra leaned forward, resting his elbows on the back of Logan's seat. "Okay, hold on," he said, his voice steady now. "Let me get this straight: you had a dream, and that dream pointed you to a spade at Marco's mansion, and now you think that's where Jordan Naudet is buried?"

47 nodded. "Yes. But it's not just about Jordan. The spade—it represents something else, something bigger. It's connected to everything Douglas has done. The corruption, the murder. It's all buried out there. And if we find it, we can bring him down."

Logan scoffed. "This is a goddamn American dream, 47. You're telling me we're going to stake our entire investigation on a vision you had in your sleep? This is what you're hanging your hopes on?"

"I saw it. I saw the mansion. I saw the land. I saw the spade," he said, his voice steady but intense. "It's all connected. The spade—it's the key. It's a symbol, and it leads directly to the mansion. There's something buried there, and I'm sure that's where Naudet's body is hidden. Or maybe it's just the proof I need to tie everything together. Either way, Marco Douglas doesn't want anyone to find out, but we're going to. And I don't care how much it takes."

Rudra glanced at him from the passenger seat. "You sure this is the right lead? We've chased a lot of wrong ones before. I just want to know that we're not walking into another trap."

47 met his gaze, the fire in his eyes unwavering. "I'm sure. This isn't a guess. This isn't speculation. I know it."

47 gripped the wheel tighter, his jaw clenched. "I didn't ask for this dream. It just happened. But I can't ignore it. Everything in me is telling me that we're on the right track. Trust me, Logan. Just this once, trust me."

Logan remained silent, still staring out the window as the car sped down the winding road leading to Marco Douglas's estate. The tension between them was palpable. It wasn't unusual for Logan to doubt 47 when things got out of hand—he always did, just as Rudra did. But that didn't stop 47 from pushing forward. This wasn't the time for doubts, not when they were so close to uncovering the truth.

## Forty Seven (47)

Rudra broke the silence, his voice surprisingly calm. "Look, Logan, I get where you're coming from. I really do. This sounds insane. But... maybe we've come this far because we've been willing to chase the impossible. We didn't get to this point by ignoring leads, no matter how strange they seemed. We kept pushing, kept following the clues, even when they didn't make sense. And right now, this—this feels like the next clue."

Logan finally turned to face them both, his eyes narrowing. "And what happens when we get to this mansion and find nothing but more dead ends? What happens then?"

47 glanced at Logan, his expression hardening with resolve. "Then we keep looking. But I know we're not walking into a dead end. I know this is the next step. This is it, Logan. We can't back down now."

There was no more argument. Logan just exhaled sharply and turned back to the window. He didn't need to say anything more. 47 knew he was in for the ride, whether he fully believed in it or not.

The car was silent for a moment, each of them processing the weight of 47's words.

Logan broke the silence. "I trust you, man. Let's do this."

The drive to Marco Douglas's mansion felt like a stretch of time and space where everything else faded away—except for the thought gnawing at 47's mind. The hum of the engine was the only sound filling the car, a rhythm that seemed almost too steady for the chaos they were about to dive into. His heart was still racing from the vision he had had earlier, the image of the mansion, the spade, the earth—everything had become clearer. But, of course, clarity came with its own weight. The more he thought about it, the more convinced he became that they were onto something much bigger than they had originally anticipated.

Soon, the car reached the outskirts of the mansion, a massive, looming structure surrounded by tall, iron gates and expansive grounds. The mansion stood like a sentinel, silent and foreboding, the very air around it heavy with secrets. The place looked even more ominous up close, its windows dark, its towering façade mocking them with the enormity of its silence. It was a fortress, designed to intimidate, to hide, to protect whatever darkness lay within.

The mansion loomed ahead, its silhouette growing larger with every passing moment. The sun had barely risen, casting a soft golden light over the sprawling estate, but the massive structure stood like a shadow—silent, imposing, and cold.

47's grip on the steering wheel tightened again as the car approached the gates. He could feel the weight of the moment—the weight of everything they had

## Forty Seven (47)

been through, everything they had sacrificed—and everything that still lay ahead.

"Alright," 47 said, his voice quiet but determined. "This is it. We'll park here and walk the rest of the way. Keep your eyes peeled. We don't know who's watching."

Logan nodded, checking his weapons discreetly. Rudra looked out at the mansion, his brow furrowed as he processed everything they had just discussed. The air around them seemed to thicken, tension seeping into every corner of the car as they pulled up to the gates.

47 could feel the pull of the place, the weight of its secrets. His heart pounded in his chest as they parked the car near a patch of trees, hidden from view. They had to be careful—if they were seen, it would all be over. This wasn't just about finding answers; it was about exposing the truth and taking down Marco Douglas, once and for all.

They exited the car quietly, their footsteps muffled against the dirt. 47 quickly surveyed the area, his eyes darting from the mansion to the surrounding grounds. There was no immediate danger. Yet.

"We need to head for the back," 47 said, his voice low. "That's where the land is open. That's where I saw the spade. The truth is buried there."

Gaurav Rajpurohit

# The Buried Truth

The moon hung low in the night sky, casting a pale light over the vast expanse of Marco Douglas's estate. The mansion, a looming structure of cold stone and glass, sat silently behind them, its windows reflecting the dull glow of the stars. The three of them—47, Logan, and Rudra—moved swiftly but cautiously, their footsteps muffled by the soft earth beneath them. The only sounds that accompanied them were the distant rustling of the trees and the occasional beep of the metal detector in Logan's hands.

They had come here for one reason: to uncover the truth. The dream, the spade, the buried secrets—everything had led them to this point. Now, with the detector in hand, they were about to find what they had been searching for. The dirt, the earth, the darkness—it was all about to give up its secrets.

"Stay low," 47 whispered, his voice barely audible as they neared the back of the mansion, the area where he was certain the truth lay buried.

Logan nodded, his eyes scanning the surroundings with sharp precision. He moved the metal detector slowly over the ground, careful not to make any unnecessary noise. His fingers were nimble, expertly handling the device, as it beeped occasionally, signaling that they were getting closer to something important.

It took a few moments, but then the metal detector gave a sharp beep. Logan paused, looking up at 47. "Got something."

They worked in unison, each of them focused on the task at hand. It felt like hours before the detector finally gave a solid signal—a clear, loud beep that echoed in the stillness.

47 knelt down beside Logan, his heart pounding in his chest. "Dig. Let's see what's beneath the surface."

The ground was soft, the soil easily disturbed. Logan began to dig, his movements swift but careful, as though he had done this a hundred times before. The tension in the air grew thicker as they worked, the silence between them charged with anticipation.

And then, after what felt like an eternity, Logan's shovel struck something hard. He froze for a moment, eyes wide.

"Over here," Logan said, crouching down and pointing to a patch of earth. "This is it."

47 didn't hesitate. He moved forward, his heart pounding in his chest. The vision of the mansion,

## Forty Seven (47)

the spade, and the buried secrets was all too vivid in his mind. He had to trust his instincts now. There was no turning back.

Rudra, ever the skeptic, stood a few steps behind, his arms crossed, eyes narrowing as he surveyed their surroundings. He had never been a fan of blindly following hunches, but he had learned to trust 47's gut over the years, even when the path seemed unclear.

As Logan continued to dig, his shovel striking the earth with deliberate force, 47 stood watch, his mind racing. What were they about to uncover? What did the spade symbolize? And why had God—through his inexplicable dream—led him here? There were too many questions, but he had no time for them. He had to focus.

The ground was soft, much easier to dig through than they had expected. It wasn't long after the sound of Logan's shovel hitting something solid broke the silence. Logan froze, his breath steady but quickening with anticipation.

"We've got something," Logan said, his voice low, almost reverent. He began to clear the dirt away with quick, practiced movements. The hole deepened, the earth giving way to something hidden beneath the surface.

The three of them worked together, the tension mounting with every scoop of dirt that was removed. As the hole widened, the shape of something metallic emerged. It was unmistakable—a metal box, weathered and tarnished by time, its surface scratched and covered in dirt. But it was there. The truth was about to be revealed.

"Careful," 47 warned, his voice strained with urgency. "We don't know what's inside. Let's be cautious."

Logan didn't hesitate. He reached down, carefully lifting the box from the hole, his fingers trembling slightly as he held it in his hands. The air around them seemed to grow heavier, as though the earth itself was holding its breath. 47's heart raced as he watched Logan lift the box.

Then, with a soft hiss, Logan pried the box open. Inside, nestled among a tangle of old papers and shredded fabric, was something that made 47's blood run cold. A torn, zippered Bible.

"That's Jordan's," 47 muttered under his breath, his voice barely audible. The torn edges, the familiar gold lettering on the cover—it was unmistakable. Jordan Naudet's Bible.

47's mind flashed back to the countless details he had about Jordan, to the man's unwavering faith, his dedication to his beliefs, and the way he carried

## Forty Seven (47)

that Bible everywhere he went. It was a symbol of everything Jordan had stood for—and now, here it was, buried in the dirt beneath Marco Douglas's estate.

"What the hell?" Rudra asked, his eyes wide with shock. "That's... that's insane."

Logan stood frozen for a moment, the Bible still clutched in his hands. Then, with a sharp breath, he turned to 47. "This... this is it. This is the breakthrough we've been waiting for."

47's mind spun. The Bible. It didn't make sense at first. Why would Jordan's Bible be buried here, with a spade, beneath Marco's mansion? But then, the pieces started to fall into place. Marco had been trying to bury Jordan's memory, to erase him, to hide the truth. The Bible had been Jordan's last connection to the world—to the truth, to his faith—and now it had been buried, as if the man's very soul was being buried along with it.

"It's a message," 47 whispered, the realization dawning on him. "This is a message. Marco couldn't just kill him. He had to erase everything that Jordan stood for. He buried him here, and he buried his faith. But it's still here. It's still part of the truth."

He reached out, taking the Bible from Logan's hands, his fingers brushing the torn pages as he flipped through it. The pages were yellowed with age, fragile from time of wear, but they still held the imprint of Jordan's life. 47's breath caught as his eyes scanned the pages.

47's voice was barely a whisper as he stared at the box in his hands. "Now, we end this."

"We've got him," 47 said quietly, a smile creeping onto his face for the first time in days.

But they weren't done yet. They had to get out of here. They had to make sure that Marco Douglas didn't get away with this.

"We need to go," 47 said, looking up at Logan and Rudra. "We've got the proof. Now we make sure the world sees it."

They nodded, and without another word, they began the long journey back to the car, their hearts lighter, but their mission far from over.

There, scrawled in the margins, were notes. Small, barely legible writings, the kind of personal thoughts Jordan would jot down when no one was looking. 47 could feel the weight of the words, the silent plea for understanding, for justice. It was as though Jordan had left behind a final message for them.

"God has helped me," 47 whispered, his voice thick with emotion as he looked up at Logan and Rudra. "God has helped me."

## Forty Seven (47)

Logan and Rudra exchanged a glance, both of them taken aback by the significance of the moment. They had been searching for so long, following so many leads, and now, here it was—the final piece of the puzzle. Jordan had been right. The truth was out there, buried beneath the surface, waiting to be uncovered.

"We need to get out of here," Logan said, his voice steady but urgent. "We've got what we need. Let's get back to the car and figure out our next move."

47 nodded, his eyes still fixed on the torn Bible in his hands. He couldn't explain it, but he could feel the weight of the moment. Everything they had fought for, everything they had struggled to uncover, was here. In his hands.

"We have to tell the world," 47 said, his voice low but determined. "We can't let this be buried again. Marco can't hide from this. Not anymore."

They moved quickly, gathering their tools and the metal detector, and retracing their steps toward the car. But as they moved through the shadows, 47 couldn't shake the feeling that they had uncovered more than just a body, more than just a torn Bible. They had uncovered a truth that would change everything.

As they drove away from the mansion, the weight of the moment pressed down on 47. He held the torn

Bible close to him, knowing that it was the key to everything. It was the last connection to Jordan, to the man who had been buried—literally and figuratively—beneath Marco Douglas's lies.

And now, with this Bible in his hands, 47 knew they had everything they needed. They had the evidence, they had the truth. The world was about to know what had happened to Jordan Naudet. Marco Douglas could run, but he couldn't hide anymore.

"God has helped me," 47 whispered again, the words a prayer, a vow, a promise. He had found the truth. And he wasn't going to stop until it was brought into the light.

# The Unmasking

The night had fallen heavy upon the three men. They were now back at 47's flat, standing around the cluttered table, their minds racing with everything they had just uncovered. The Bible, the spade, the body—it all made sense now. Jordan Naudet's last words had been buried under the very ground that Marco Douglas called home. But they knew better than to celebrate. The real battle was far from over.

47 stood, his hands clenched at his sides, staring down at the torn Bible that had revealed so much. The more he thought about it, the clearer it became: Marco Douglas was behind Jordan's death. The evidence had been buried for so long, hidden beneath layers of lies and manipulation, but 47 had found it. God had given him the guidance, and he wasn't about to let it slip away. But there was more to be done. Much more.

Rudra's voice interrupted his thoughts. "Don't shout, Edward. Douglas will find out. He's not stupid. He'll know what we've uncovered."

47's eyes narrowed, and his jaw tightened. He knew Rudra was right. Marco Douglas was powerful, ruthless, and always one step ahead of everyone else. He had built an empire on lies and deceit. But what Rudra didn't understand, what neither Logan nor Rudra could fully grasp, was the depth of 47's resolve.

"He can come to know of it all he wants," 47 muttered, his voice low, almost cold. "He's not getting away with it this time. He's already too far gone, and now I've got him."

47 turned toward the table, his fingers brushing the surface of the torn Bible one last time before he reached for his laptop. The room had a heavy silence to it, as though the air itself was holding its breath. Logan and Rudra exchanged uncertain looks before moving closer, their eyes on the screen as 47 opened up his case files.

"I'm going to match his fingerprints," 47 said, his tone resolute, the fire in his eyes burning brighter. He turned to the others. "Marco Douglas's fingerprints were all over the crime scene—the spade, the body. I'm going to match them, and then I'll finally have the proof. We can end this."

Logan crossed his arms, studying his friend closely. "You're sure about this, right? You're not just chasing ghosts?"

47's fingers were already flying over the keyboard, inputting the data. "I don't chase ghosts, Logan. I

## Forty Seven (47)

chase the truth." His voice was unwavering, and for the first time in a long while, he felt the clarity he had been missing for days. It wasn't just about solving a murder anymore. It was about justice, redemption, and holding Marco Douglas accountable for the darkness he had unleashed.

Rudra stepped forward, sensing the tension in the room. "So, what's the next step? What do you need us to do?"

47 didn't take his eyes off the screen. "You two need to gather the rest of the evidence—the spade, the body, anything else we can tie to Douglas. I'm going to run the fingerprint analysis."

The room fell into an uneasy quiet as Logan and Rudra moved to gather the remaining pieces of the puzzle. Their steps echoed in the stillness, but 47 remained at the laptop, his mind racing through every step of the investigation. The last few days had been a whirlwind—betrayal, confusion, and a relentless chase for the truth. But now, he was closer than ever to catching the man who had destroyed everything Jordan Naudet had stood for.

The hours dragged on. Every second felt like an eternity as 47 waited for the analysis to run. His mind wandered back to that moment in the dirt, when they had uncovered Jordan's Bible, when he had finally understood the message. It had all led to this. Douglas was ruthless. He had killed before, and he would kill again if given the chance. But now, 47 was armed with the one thing Douglas couldn't escape: the truth.

The beep of the computer brought him back to reality. 47 leaned forward, his eyes locked onto the screen as the fingerprint match process completed. The results were almost instantaneous. There it was. A perfect match. Marco Douglas.

"Got him," 47 said, his voice steady but filled with quiet triumph. "His fingerprints are all over the spade and the body. He did this."

Logan and Rudra moved back toward him, their faces lit by the glow of the screen. They exchanged a glance, understanding the gravity of the moment. This wasn't just a breakthrough. This was the final piece of the puzzle.

"So what now?" Rudra asked, his voice thick with anticipation.

47 stood, his eyes blazing with determination. "Now we go after him. No more running, no more hiding. We bring him in."

The weight of the words hung in the air. Marco Douglas, the man who had orchestrated Jordan Naudet's death, who had manipulated everyone around him, was finally going to be held accountable. There was no turning back now. 47

## Forty Seven (47)

was done waiting. He had the evidence, he had the truth, and it was time for justice to prevail.

"Logan, get the warrant. Rudra, you're with me. We're going to Douglas's mansion. He's going to try to run, but he won't get far. Not this time."

Rudra nodded, grabbing his gear and heading toward the door. Logan was already on his phone, working to secure the warrant they would need to confront Marco Douglas. But 47 didn't need a piece of paper to tell him what was right. He already knew what had to be done.

As they drove toward Marco Douglas's mansion, 47's mind raced. He thought of Jordan, of the man who had trusted the truth, who had believed in justice until the very end. Jordan had carried that Bible for a reason, a symbol of faith, of truth. And now, 47 had become the instrument of that truth.

They arrived at the mansion under the cover of darkness, the lights of the sprawling estate casting long shadows across the driveway. The massive gates stood in front of them, imposing and silent. 47's eyes narrowed as he surveyed the area.

"This is it," 47 said, his voice a low murmur. "We move fast. No mistakes."

Logan and Rudra nodded, their faces set in grim determination. They knew what was at stake here, what had been lost, and what was about to be gained.

They approached the gates, moving quietly but quickly, their footsteps muffled by the thick grass beneath them. The mansion loomed ahead, its towering form a symbol of Marco Douglas's power and corruption. But that power was about to come crashing down.

47's heart pounded in his chest as they moved closer to the mansion. The air was thick with tension. He had never been more certain of anything in his life. They had the proof. They had the truth. And now, Marco Douglas was going to face the consequences of his actions.

As they reached the door, 47 gave the signal. Logan and Rudra moved to either side, their weapons drawn, ready for whatever might come next. 47 didn't wait. He slammed his fist against the door, the sound echoing through the quiet night.

"Marco Douglas!" he shouted, his voice cutting through the silence like a blade. "We know what you've done. Come out now!"

For a moment, there was nothing but the silence of the night. Then, the sound of footsteps. Heavy, deliberate, but unmistakably the footsteps of a man who knew the end was near.

## Forty Seven (47)

Marco Douglas stepped into view, his face a mask of cold indifference. But 47 could see it in his eyes—the flicker of panic, the recognition that the game was up.

"You think you can stop me?" Marco sneered, his voice dripping with contempt. "You think you can expose me and walk away unscathed?"

47 stepped forward, his eyes locked on Douglas's. "It's over, Marco. You're done. You killed Jordan, and now you're going to pay for it. There's nowhere left for you to run."

Marco's eyes narrowed, his lips curling into a twisted smile. "You think you've won, don't you? You think you've got the truth on your side. But I've been in control this whole time. I'll make sure you never get out of here alive."

But 47 wasn't afraid. He had already won. The truth was on his side, and nothing Marco could say or could do to change that.

With a signal to Logan and Rudra, 47 closed in on Marco. The chase was over.

# The Fall of Marco Douglas

The city felt different the next morning, quieter somehow. The morning air, usually thick with the chaos of the day ahead, seemed to have settled into a kind of heavy calm. Perhaps it was the kind of peace that followed a storm—a peace before the inevitable consequences caught up with them. And for Marco Douglas, the storm was just beginning.

47 sat at the kitchen table in his flat, staring at the cup of coffee before him. His fingers were drumming rhythmically against the ceramic, but his mind was miles away, replaying the events of the night before. The confrontation with Marco Douglas had gone smoother than expected, but there was something unsettling in the way Douglas had acted when he was caught—almost resigned, as if he had been waiting for the inevitable moment when his empire would crumble.

His admission, once they had cornered him, had been chilling. Marco Douglas, the man who had built his empire on power and control, had admitted to everything—Jordan Naudet's murder, the manipulation of the investigation, and the twisted exchange of Naudet's body with the shooter

## Forty Seven (47)

in the forest. His confession came not with the fury of a man caught but with the emptiness of someone who knew it was too late for redemption.

"I had to do it," Douglas had said when they confronted him. "Naudet was always a threat. You wouldn't understand the stakes. The world doesn't work on ideals, 47. It works on power. And I had the power." His eyes had hardened when he said it, as if he truly believed that his survival justified everything.

But that was before the law caught up with him.

47's phone buzzed, snapping him out of his reverie. It was Logan.

**"We're at the courthouse. You need to be here. It's starting."**

The words sent a rush of urgency through him. The end was near. The case, which had seemed to be hopeless just a few days ago, was now in its final stages. Marco Douglas was going to face justice.

---

The courthouse was packed, a crowd gathered outside the massive stone building. It felt as though the city itself was holding its breath, waiting for the downfall of one of its most powerful figures. The media was buzzing, cameras flashing as reporters jockeyed for position, eager to capture every moment of the trial that was about to unfold.

47 arrived at the courthouse, his footsteps steady, each one echoing off the cold marble floor of the lobby. He knew what he was about to witness was history in the making. It wasn't every day that a man as influential as Marco Douglas was brought to his knees by the truth. But today was different. Today, the truth was going to be heard.

Logan and Rudra were already inside the courtroom, their expressions serious as they sat in the front row. The air was thick with tension, and the murmur of conversation among the crowd died down when the judge entered. The gavel struck, and the trial began.

The defense team, a group of sharp-suited lawyers with cold, calculating eyes, wasted no time in presenting their arguments. They tried to paint Douglas as a victim of circumstance, a man who had been forced to make difficult decisions in the cutthroat world of business. They tried to claim that the murder of Jordan Naudet was a misunderstanding, a tragic accident that had spiraled out of control.

But 47 wasn't fooled. He had the evidence—hard, irrefutable evidence that tied Marco Douglas to Naudet's death. The fingerprints, the torn Bible, the spade—they all pointed to him. There was no escaping it.

## Forty Seven (47)

As the prosecution called its first witness, a slow sense of inevitability began to settle over the courtroom. One by one, they presented their case, laying out the facts, connecting the dots, and exposing Marco Douglas's web of lies. The courtroom was silent as the witnesses spoke, and 47 could feel the weight of every word.

Finally, it was time for Douglas to take the stand.

He walked into the courtroom with the kind of confidence that only a man who had lived his life manipulating others could possess. His suit was impeccably tailored, his hair neatly combed, but there was a weariness in his eyes now. The mask of the powerful businessman had cracked, and in its place was a man who knew his time had run out.

"Mr. Douglas," the prosecutor began, his voice steady. "You stand accused of the murder of Jordan Naudet, the tampering of evidence, and the manipulation of an ongoing investigation. How do you plead?"

Douglas's voice was calm, too calm. "Not guilty."

But it was a hollow statement, one that the prosecutor quickly dismantled.

The trial went on for hours, the evidence mounting against Douglas. His lawyers tried to deflect, tried to discredit the findings, but nothing could stop the tide. The fingerprints matched. The Bible was found near the body. The metal detector had uncovered the truth. And most damning of all, Marco Douglas's own confession—made to 47 and his team—was read aloud in court.

"Let me make something clear," the prosecutor said, turning to address the jury. "Marco Douglas exchanged the dead body of Jordan Naudet in the forest with the shooter of Naudet. His motive was simple—power. He couldn't afford to let Naudet, a man who stood for justice, stand in the way of his empire. So he killed him. And then he tried to bury the truth, literally, with the body."

Douglas's eyes flickered for a moment, but he said nothing. He sat there, his posture still proud, but his silence spoke volumes.

Finally, the defense stood, its final witness about to be called. It was Marco himself.

"Mr. Douglas," the defense attorney said, addressing the court, "do you have anything to say for yourself?"

The room went quiet as Marco Douglas stood. His hands trembled slightly as he adjusted his tie, his gaze scanning the courtroom. He looked at the jury, then at the prosecutor, and finally, his eyes locked onto 47.

"I'll tell you what happened," Douglas began, his voice steady but strained. "I did what I had to do. I

## Forty Seven (47)

made choices that no one else could make. People like Jordan Naudet—people who believe in ideals—get in the way of progress. They want to fix the world, but they don't understand how the world really works. I did what I had to do to survive."

His eyes lingered on 47 for a moment, a flicker of recognition passing between them. 47's gaze never wavered.

"I never wanted to kill him," Marco continued, his voice cracking slightly. "But in this world, you either kill or be killed. I chose to kill."

The courtroom held its breath. For a moment, it seemed as if Marco Douglas might find some last shred of dignity in his confession. But there was none. The damage had been done, and the weight of his words sank deep into the room. His admission was not one of remorse, but of cold, calculated justification.

"Thank you, Mr. Douglas," the prosecutor said, his tone dismissive. He turned to the jury. "You have all the facts. The evidence is clear. The truth has been laid bare. There is no doubt. We ask you to return a verdict of guilty."

The jury deliberated for what felt like an eternity, but when they returned, their decision was swift and without hesitation. Guilty on all charges.

The courtroom erupted into a chorus of murmurs and whispers. But 47 felt nothing but a sense of closure. Justice had been served. Marco Douglas, once untouchable, was now nothing more than a criminal—a man brought to justice by the very truth he had tried to bury.

The judge's gavel struck, and Marco Douglas was led away in handcuffs, his face a mixture of disbelief and anger. But there was no escape for him now. The law had caught up with him, and the consequences of his actions would follow him for the rest of his life.

As 47 left the courtroom, the weight of the last few days seemed to lift from his shoulders. It was over. But in his heart, he knew that the fight for justice never truly ended. It was a constant battle—a battle he would continue to fight for as long as he had breath in his body.

And as he walked out into the daylight, the weight of the torn Bible still heavy in his bag, 47 knew that the truth would always be his greatest weapon.

# The Final Farewell

The heavy scent of fresh-cut flowers lingered in the air as 47 stood by the edge of the open grave, his hands clenched tightly at his sides. The crowd had gathered, and though the sun shone brightly overhead, there was a sense of muted sorrow in the atmosphere. Jordan Naudet's funeral had become a quiet affair, attended by those who had known him in life, his friends, colleagues, and even some former adversaries who, in the end, had come to respect him.

The mourners stood in solemn silence as the priest recited the final prayers, his voice steady and comforting. But to 47, the words were distant. His mind, as it often did during moments of reflection, wandered back to the investigation, to the moments before Naudet's death, and to the bittersweet conclusion of the case.

It was over now. Marco Douglas was in jail, his empire shattered. The truth had been unearthed. But the cost had been high. Jordan Naudet was gone. And though justice had been served, it felt like a hollow victory. A piece of the puzzle had been put together, but there was a part of 47 that still felt incomplete.

Standing next to him were Rudra and Logan, the two brothers who had stood by him throughout the case. They didn't speak, but their presence was a comfort—silent companions who understood the weight of what had just happened. They had seen the depth of 47's struggle, his doubts, his fears, and his persistence. And now, as they all watched the casket slowly lower into the earth, they could feel the weight of the loss.

The card 47 held in his hand was simple, a white rectangle with a single line of text: *"May his soul rest in God's feet."* It was a message from one of Jordan's closest friends—a final sentiment of peace for a man who had spent much of his life fighting for justice, even when it cost him everything.

As 47 read the words again, he felt a small knot tighten in his chest. He had never known Jordan Naudet personally, but he had come to admire him. The man had been driven, not by ambition or the desire for wealth, but by a deep, unshakable belief in doing what was right. And in the end, that belief had cost him his life. But 47 knew that Jordan had lived his life on his terms, standing firm in his convictions, even when faced with the brutal reality of a world that often rewarded the wrong people.

**"He deserved better,"** Logan said quietly, breaking the silence. The words hung in the air for a moment, and 47 nodded in agreement.

## Forty Seven (47)

"He did," 47 replied, his voice hoarse. He had spoken more in the past few days than he had in weeks, but today, he found himself struggling to find the right words.

The priest continued his prayers, but 47's thoughts were elsewhere. His mind kept drifting back to that final moment in the woods—the moment when they had uncovered Jordan's body, hidden away, buried in the earth as if he was just another casualty of a world that cared little for justice. The spade, the Bible, the final moments of Jordan's life... everything had been leading to this. But it felt like there was so much more left unsaid.

"Does anyone ever really get closure from something like this?" Rudra asked, his voice low. He had been quiet throughout the proceedings, but now, as the words settled, 47 turned to look at him.

**"I don't think you ever get real closure,"** 47 said, his eyes meeting Rudra's. **"Not from something like this. But you find a way to live with it."**

Rudra's eyes flickered as he looked down at the ground, nodding slowly. They all understood what 47 meant. The world didn't offer easy answers. The truth, when it came, was often messy, tangled in a web of deceit and compromise. And even when you uncovered it, there was no satisfaction, no sense of complete triumph. There was only the weight of knowing that you had done what you could, and that sometimes, that had to be enough.

The funeral continued, the mourners filing past the grave, offering their last respects. Some whispered prayers, others simply nodded, their eyes filled with sorrow. But no one spoke of the case, of the investigation that had led them here. There were no accolades for 47, no applause for his persistence. It was a moment of quiet reflection, of respect for a man who had given everything in the name of justice.

As the last few mourners left, 47 remained standing, his gaze fixed on the grave. The wind had picked up slightly, rustling the leaves of the nearby trees. It was a peaceful sound, a reminder that life went on, no matter what.

Logan stepped forward, his hand resting gently on 47's shoulder. **"You did what you could, 47. He wouldn't want you to carry this forever."**

47 glanced at him, his eyes tired but determined. **"It's not about what he would want. It's about what's right."**

Logan didn't argue. There were no more words left to say.

---

Later that evening, as 47 sat alone in his apartment, the weight of the day finally caught up with him.

## Forty Seven (47)

The funeral had been a small, intimate affair, but the truth behind it—the case, the murder, the lies—was anything but simple. He looked at the Bible on the table in front of him, the very same one that had played a key role in the investigation. It had been there in the ground, lying next to Jordan's body, torn and weathered. It had guided him, even when his own faith in the investigation had faltered. And now, as he gazed at it, he wondered what it had meant, what it still meant in the aftermath.

His phone buzzed on the table, pulling him from his thoughts. It was a message from Rudra.

**"You good?"**

47 stared at the message for a moment before responding.

**"Yeah. Just thinking."**

The reply came almost instantly.

**"It's been a hell of a ride, hasn't it?"**

47 smiled faintly, though there was no joy in it. It had been a hell of a ride. But now, as the dust settled, there was a sense of finality. He had uncovered the truth. He had fought for justice. But in the end, it was just one more case. One more life lost in a world that didn't always value the right things.

"**It's over now,**" he typed back. "**We did what we had to do.**"

The message lingered on the screen for a moment before Rudra's reply came through.

"**Yeah. And Naudet can rest now.**"

47 put the phone down, his eyes drifting once again to the Bible on the table. He picked it up slowly, his fingers tracing the torn cover. There were so many questions, so many things left unanswered. But one thing was certain—Jordan Naudet's death had not been in vain. The truth had come to light, and for that, he could find some peace.

As the night stretched on, 47 leaned back in his chair, his eyes closing briefly. He had done what he could. The weight of the investigation, the lies, the death, the betrayal—everything had been laid bare. It had taken everything he had, but in the end, justice had been served. The world might not be any less corrupt, but it was a little bit more honest now.

And for Jordan Naudet, that was enough.

---

The funeral had been a day of closure for many, but for 47, it was simply another chapter in a life spent seeking the truth. And as the days stretched into weeks, and the case faded into the past, one thing remained clear in his mind: No matter how many

## Forty Seven (47)

cases he solved, no matter how many truths he uncovered, the world would always have another story to tell. And he would always be there, ready to listen.

Because for men like 47, the search for justice never truly ended.

It simply started again.

# Epilogue: A Full Circle

James Bean sat in the dimly lit room, the flicker of the TV screen casting shadows across the walls. The closing credits of the movie rolled by, but his gaze was fixed on the final scene—a funeral, simple but poignant. The last note of music hung in the air like a final sigh of a chapter closed. He had seen it before, the movie about the Naudet case, the unsolved mystery, the chase, the dead body in the forest, and the spade. But tonight, it wasn't just the story that caught his attention. It was the card. The same card that had been tucked away in the back of his own collection for years.

"May his soul rest in God's feet. UP."

A card like no other, with its simple message and unassuming design. Yet it was no accident that it had found its way into the collection of someone who had spent so many years collecting pieces of the world's strange and complicated puzzle. James had long known that the world had a way of connecting people, events, and objects in ways that defied logic. And now, as he stared at the screen, something shifted in him. There was more to the story than he had realized.

## Forty Seven (47)

Rising from his worn armchair, he crossed the room and approached the shelf that housed his collection of cards—vintage postcards, handwritten notes, mementos from forgotten eras, and objects of profound mystery. Each card told a story. Each piece was a fragment of something greater. He ran his fingers over the shelf, each item steeped in history, until his hand rested on the edge of the small wooden box. He opened it carefully, his heart beating a little faster as he reached for the card.

The one with the simple inscription. The one that had crossed his path years ago, and that had led him into a spiral of questions he never quite found answers to. The one that had somehow come into his possession after an obscure auction he'd attended on a whim. The one that, as he now realized, had a connection to a case he had followed from a distance but had never truly understood.

James smiled, a soft, knowing smile. The world was smaller than it seemed. Everything, every strange encounter, every discarded clue, had somehow come together in a single moment. He placed the card back into its rightful spot on the shelf, the weight of its presence now more meaningful than it had ever been before. It had been a symbol of curiosity then; now, it was a symbol of closure.

The screen flickered off, and James turned away from the television. His life had been a series of quiet observations, collecting stories and bits of the world that no one else seemed to notice. He wasn't a detective like 47 or a key player in some grand scheme of justice. But in his own way, James had always been a participant in the stories of others, someone who quietly pieced together the fragments that others discarded.

He walked over to the window and looked out at the night sky. The world outside was still, the streets bathed in the soft glow of streetlights, but within him, there was a sense of movement, of purpose. The investigation into the death of Jordan Naudet had ended, but in a way, the case was still alive within him. It had left its mark, and for reasons he couldn't fully explain, it had connected to his own story in a way he hadn't anticipated.

His thoughts drifted to the man who had solved the case, 47. He had done what so many others couldn't—he had found the truth buried deep within layers of lies and deceit. James had watched him from the side-lines, fascinated by his tenacity and his ability to see through the smoke and mirrors that the world often relied on. It was rare to find someone who cared so deeply about justice, so consumed by the search for truth, even when it meant risking everything.

James had never been like that. He hadn't been driven by the need to solve a case or to uncover the hidden truths that lurked beneath the surface of life. But he respected those who were. In his own way, he admired their relentless pursuit of something greater than themselves.

The card in his collection had been a token of that admiration. It was a reminder of the complexities of the world, of the stories that lay just beneath the surface, waiting to be uncovered by those brave enough to seek them out. But now, as he stood there looking out at the city, he felt that the story had come full circle. The answers that had been elusive for so long had found their way to him, and he was finally ready to let go of them.

James knew that the world was full of mysteries, some solved, some still waiting for the right person to stumble upon the key. But there was no more chasing for him, no more collecting clues that wouldn't lead anywhere. His role in this particular story had ended, and it was time for him to move on, to find the next chapter in his own life.

But as he stood there, something whispered in his mind—a soft, persistent thought that refused to be silenced. It wasn't a question of whether or not there were more stories to uncover. The question, it seemed, was whether or not he was willing to keep going. To keep looking. To keep finding.

And for the first time in a long while, he wasn't sure if he was ready to stop.

Weeks passed. The funeral of Jordan Naudet had come and gone, leaving behind a trail of questions and revelations. The final resolution of the case had come as a bittersweet victory. 47 had done what he could, and the truth had been revealed. But James Bean, though not part of the investigation itself, had continued to think about the story. Something about it had captured his attention, perhaps more than he realized. He found himself revisiting old notes, reading up on the history of the Naudet family, researching more about Marco Douglas, and his empire. He wasn't sure what he was looking for, but he couldn't shake the feeling that there was more to the story, more pieces left scattered, waiting to be discovered.

One evening, as James walked through the city's quiet streets, he found himself near an old bookstore he hadn't visited in years. It was a small place, tucked between two larger buildings, with faded signs hanging above the door. Something about it seemed familiar. Maybe it was the promise of forgotten stories, of old books that whispered secrets to those who took the time to listen.

He stepped inside, greeted by the musty scent of leather and paper. The dim lighting and rows upon rows of dusty volumes created an atmosphere of nostalgia. James wandered through the aisles, running his fingers across the spines of books that had long since been forgotten by the world.

Then, near the back of the store, a particular book caught his eye. It was an old, leather-bound journal, its cover worn from years of use. As he opened it, he realized it was a collection of letters. At first, he thought it was just a random assortment of words, but as he flipped through the pages, something stopped him. There, in the margins, were notes written in the same handwriting as the card he had kept in his collection.

The connections were clearer now. It was as if the universe had drawn another thread, pulling him back into a world he had almost forgotten.

James smiled again, a quiet, knowing smile. It was like he was meant to find this. Like he was meant to keep searching, to keep digging. Maybe it was just curiosity. Maybe it was fate. But for now, he had found something new to collect, another story to piece together.

And for the first time, James Bean realized that some stories never truly end. They simply evolve, waiting for the right person to uncover the next chapter.

And he was more than ready.

www.ingramcontent.com/pod-product-compliance
Lightning Source LLC
LaVergne TN
LVHW061543070526
838199LV00077B/6883